The Christmas Party

By
Thomas Green, Jr.

South Of Harlem Books
Atlanta, Ga.

Also by Thomas Green, Jr.

Decatur Cab
Change for A Dyme
Larry's Girls
Purple Lipstick
Tabu (with Thomas Green, Sr.)
When it Hurts So Bad
Player No More
Courting Miss Thang
Love's Home Run

The Christmas Party

Then...
<u>DECEMBER 23, 1982</u>

Prologue

Theodore Taylor spent a month's pay on the first Christmas party.

He had to spend so much money, he reasoned to his angry wife. She would have saved him so much money if he had allowed her to cook. That would come later, like in two years when money was a little tighter.

It all started as a way for Teddy to celebrate his foray into the world of Georgia politics. He had just won his first political race, a seat on Atlanta's city council, and he was making friends with many of the big shots in the city. The mayor liked him enough to have lunch one on one with him and to endorse his run. It was also a way to show off the new home he bought for his family.

Nobody knew, and probably they wouldn't have cared, how much those parties cost Teddy. But in the later years, as the 90s arrived he had figured out ways to get party favors, the food and booze, on the low-low from companies and folks that wanted it known they sponsored the event.

But no, this first one, it was a celebration. Teddy didn't want his wife, the tall, slender and sexy, Verdie Taylor, to do anything but have fun.

"This is the party of the year. Like harvest for the slaves back in the day, baby. Ain't no working in the kitchen. You did that for Thanksgiving. Relax."

"Harvest for slaves? You are one bolt loose from being nuts," Verdie told him.

He grabbed her into a bear hug like he did damn near everyday of their lives together and said, "I'm nuts and you love me, so what you saying?"

Telling Verdie not to cook when people were coming over was like asking O.J. Simpson to leave white women alone, just wasn't going to happen.

Teddy's wife was the master of the kitchen. So despite Teddy brokering a deal with the local Chinese restaurant to make a bundle of wings and lo mien, She did most of the cooking, and all of the baking. She'd make four kinds of pies, and then two apple pies that were only for her husband. Folks loved her fudge stuff, brownies and bears with icing, and her amazing sugar cookies cut into Christmas trees, angels, reindeer, snowmen, and candy canes.

That first party was held in great weather; in Atlanta a party could be doomed by weather being less than 50 degrees as darkness came. It was warm, damn near seventy, at the beginning of the month. By the time Christmas came, most folks hadn't taken out their parkas or snow coats yet.

Teddy sent out hundreds of invites; to everyone he knew and some he didn't like much. Dozens of folks showed.

As people arrived, though, Verdie thought the gang of folks that did show would be too much for their new home to handle. She worried that there wouldn't be enough finger food to go around. So she fired up her kitchen and, while wearing an apron over her elegant Christmas dress, she exudes the aura of a seasoned host and lady of the house. (By year three the date was set, Teddy's party was on Dec. 23, and word of mouth made and no need to mail invites.)

It all worked out fine. There was plenty of food; with the hot wings, fried wings, Lo Mien, chips with three different dips and the chicken salad and tossed green salad Verdie added. The booze was what ran out. Despite four cases of beer, a gallon of all the essential liquors, rum, vodka, gin and of course Hennessy, there was nothing left over. (That never happened again...to Verdie's unnerving, the parties from then on would have enough booze to supply a club for a month.)

At midnight Teddy took center stage in the room next to the tree. He cut off the music and then tapped a spoon on his glass of Champagne. As everyone gathers into the room quieted, Teddy cleared his throat to speak.

"Verdie, baby, the wife of all this, come hither."

"Hither? Nigger, please," said on of Teddy's oldest friends, Jon Penny.

"Hold up, I got class. Just ask your wife!"

"Hey!"

"Okay, okay, enough of Jon's fine wife. My dear friends and family, I'd like to propose a toast on this most special occasion we call Christmas. This is the season of giving and I'd like to give each and everyone my home, well not exactly everyone, especially if you didn't vote for me."

Teddy reveled in the laughter from the guests.

"But no, really, this is the first Taylor Christmas party in our new home, and it was something my mother started as we grew up on the south side of Chicago when we couldn't afford any gifts or a tree or presents, and all that stuff that comes with the holidays. She wanted me and my brothers to realize that we had each other. And as long as we had each other, we were okay. We could have a sad and lonely Christmas, or we could choose to have fun with each other. As I said, we didn't have a lot, but we had an old record player and a whole lot of records.

"I want everyone to look around this room, and realize that this party is not about Christmas-but about us, right now, coming together as family and friends. And knowing there's no greater gift...And to that, I have a special song that I just want everybody to reflect on."

And Ted moved through the bodies and to his stereo against the wall and put a different record on.

He gently cleaned the needle, somebody yelled out, "Come on now! You holding up the party."

"Put the needle on the record, fool," somebody else said.

Ted's response was, "Nice. Jesus was born and none of you got the patience of an angel." He took his time and carried the needle over the vinyl, counting out the lines until he was at the eighth spot. Then he set the needle down.

"It better not be no damn Nate Cole."

"Nat King Cole, the man's momma named him Nat, you call him Nat King Cole," Ted corrected his mocker. He turned the sound up and announced, "Here comes the baddest rapper in the land. And if you ain't dancing I don't want to see you anymore."

Kurtis Blow's Christmas Rappin' played, nice and loud.

"This the jam right here!" Ted shouted in glee as people started to groove to the song. He grabbed Verdie from behind and spins her around to dance.

Everyone in the room laughs and breaks out into dance.

Ted, playing to the camera David held on his parents, broke out into his version of the robot.

"Teddy, this party is hittin' right," one of his friends said.

"The best is yet to come, baby."

No one left before 2 a.m., and no one left without a smile or a plate.

And thus, a tradition was born.

The Christmas Party

Now...

1

Theodore Taylor had just turned 54 the month the good Lord took him home to his reward.

He woke up on a steamy August morning to find the tie he wanted to wear was gone. His dapper son, not the one that still lives in the bedroom he grew up in, had raided his closet yet once again.

Damn it.

Teddy Taylor loved his ties; they set off his designer suits and custom made shirts. As a politician, a Georgia state senator, he felt he had to look good everyday, everyday. And that day he wanted to rock that slick brown and beige and burnt orange jammie to set off his almost beige suit with the harvest orange shirt. It was a suit that looked more Fall than summer, but he wanted to wear it, it was his prerogative, right?

Forget the fact that he had dozens of other custom made ties in his closet. He wanted that one. The other ties were older, and he damned wished his son had taken one of them. It was the principle of the matter, he fumed.

After he tugged on his slacks and the rest of his suit, he barged through the house complaining "A Black man, who works all day, can't have some shit for himself? Fuck. They can buy fucking ties like I buy mine. They got jobs. Tricia probably borrowed it, and I am using my fingers, for one of her losers that don't own a suit."

"Please?"

"Why don't y'all please me sometimes and stop touching my shit. Is this what Malcolm X had to deal with? People always touching his shit."

"That happens. You shouldn't have had a family and had lived alone. Then you wouldn't have this worry."

"I wish."

Those were Teddy Taylor's last words to his wife. In a rage, he left the house and never came back.

David heard his pop's rant. It woke him up, but since he hadn't stole any of his dad's precious ties, he stayed out of it. David check his digital clock, saw that it was a little after nine, too early for a man on his day off to be awake, and he turned over in the bed and forced sleep to come back to him.

He drove in fury. Did they think to ask first? No. Would he ever see the tie again? Probably not, unless he went out and bought the same one again.

Once again one of his loveable, spoiled-ass, sons has taken a neck tie he liked and made it disappear, he was thinking through an angry mind as he dropped his suit into the back seat of his Lexus.

"Fuck this." Teddy called his tie maker.

"I have nothing new," Reynolds pleaded. He himself just getting out of bed. "Give me some time."

"Well, I need some ties, damn it. Hook me up. Shit, I am about to go to Macy's like I ain't got no money in the bank."

"Theodore no, not that," Reynolds mocked. "No, don't do that. Seriously, okay? I will hook you up, my brother."

"I do not have time to wait for you to get out of bed and open your store. I have a meeting at 10:30."

Teddy was just walking in the mall, witnesses said. He didn't look angry. He wasn't mumbling and cursing, just strolling his way through. Then he stopped moving. No one was near him.

Tanesha Jefferson saw it happen. She was moving quickly in his direction, it was a minute to 10 a.m. and she was rushing to not be late in opening the shoe store she managed in the mall. She was still a dozen feet away when he fell. She told the cops that he looked like he was scratching his arm and chest and then he went down to his knees first and then all four before laying down.

Despite being late, she stopped to offer aid and got the fright of her life. It was her first time witnessing the death of a human being.

The funeral was a big affair; not just because a politician had passed, but because a beloved community figure was taken home much too soon. He had touched the lives of many.

2

Some people would have told you what they loved the most about Theodore Taylor's annual Christmas party was the music and the dancing...the good time.

Some would have said it was the cheer; by cheer they would be talking about the serious open bar with all kinds of liquor, and champagne, and the delicious food. And most of them loved the fact that even though they didn't *have* to bring a damn thing (many people did bring a bottle of something at least), they'd be able to drink until they dropped and eat until they'd burst.

Others, though, would say what the liked most about Teddy's Christmas party was the host himself. Teddy was a party animal and the kind of host that naturally showed everybody a good time. His secret was that he liked to have a drink and be merry.

Teddy opened his Victorian mansion with ornate cream and raspberry wood trim and dark green shingles to the world every year on December 23. Most folks didn't mark it down. They would know but the buzz, by all their friends talking about it, getting ready for it.

The Taylor home was truly a sight. The wood was freshly painted and well kept. It was a full two flights, six bedrooms and four and a half baths and a full basement Teddy used as his sanctuary. Once in the front door, the spacious foyer gave visitors a sense of welcome. Teddy put work in designing and building it, taking special care in the spacious kitchen, where he burned up some pots and pans as much as his wife. He had to have his sunken living room and he was the only person there that had ever tripped going up or down the two steps.

Many of the people that had enjoyed themselves for years at the Taylor home were now afraid to even call and offer cheer to the Mrs. Their thoughts were, if they were depressed about not having the jolly Teddy or his joyous party then she must be a mess, and so the last thing she probably needed was to be reminded that it was Christmas Time.

So nobody called as the holiday season neared. Let her mourn in peace, seemed to be the prevailing thought. And that was just what she had planned. To just chill, quietly, no fuss, and then wake up and it would be January, a new year.

Verdie used to love to do all the things involved with making the Christmas season joyous. All the decorating, all the cooking and baking

And no matter how many people in her family tell her otherwise, Verdie will forever be haunted by the fact that she, in her mind, had a fight with him before he went out the door. She was haunted for a long time by his last words, "I wish." She was tired of his complaining about what she considered petty happenings. Sure, the children were grown and still eating his stuff, using his stuff, bothering with his stuff.

No husband, no holidays, which had been her thinking since the funeral. But their children, who were molded in the shape of his thinking, were set to take up the party. Her children wanted to keep the tradition alive. They wanted to make it happen. Adam, her oldest, the main culprit when it came to taking, using, Teddy stuff, was also his mini twin. Adam was into politics, following in his father's footsteps, and he felt like he *needed* the party.

Adam had just won a seat in the city council that November, and he had his sights on mayor, a seat his daddy had never wanted for himself. Adam was promised by Teddy that at this year's party he could be introduced as a future powerbroker and that Teddy would endorse Adam's expansion into big boy's politics.

Teddy's other children had mixed emotions about continuing the tradition of their dad's party. David Taylor wanted his mother happy; and if she wasn't cool with it then he'd rather do what she'd like. Patricia Taylor was Theodore and Verdie's only girl, their middle child; his baby girl forever, Teddy would say. She didn't have that middle child problem, Teddy treated all his children the same...hard. Patricia was more in the middle. She just didn't want to have to choose. She would have been cool with not seeing everyone until Christmas Day.

3

Kurtis Blow had never been David Taylor's favorite rapper, but it just wouldn't be Christmas for David without Blow's ode to the holiday.

David was a six-footer, a good-looking, jolly kind of guy. He was in his mid twenties, single, heterosexual and never married. That combination in Atlanta was as rare as a snowflake. Everybody was taken in by his spirit and love of life. David is the assistant manager of Lollypop Music, where he has worked for six years.

David was bobbing his head. Letting the song take his mind on a trip He had the song blaring from the speakers at the CD store.

He was back at the first Christmas party his dad threw. He was seven years old at the time, and saw most of the party through the lens of his dad's 8mm home movie camera. He was given full reign of his dad's video camera.

It was the Reverend Lenny Penny and his mother's sister Bebe that gave him the most joy that year. Penny wasn't a minister yet; he was just a guy back then who work with David's dad. He was the first person to tell David dirty jokes, and, back then, he was generous with his money, always hitting David with a five dollar bill. Now, though, he tells corny jokes and he doesn't share his money with anyone.

David kept the camera on Rev. Penny and Bebe; they were making out anywhere they could. He caught them in his mother's bathroom, and in two different closets.

He smiled at the remembrance of Bebe's sexy body, those nice breasts, and the way Rev. Penny groped her.

He recalled following his dad's group. They were gathered near the basement door. The tallest and roundest of the men open the door and gestures them down into the basement. He can't recall that guy's name, he and his dad stopped hanging out in the 90s. The men were talking almost secretively as they balance brandy snifters in one hand and thick fragrant cigars in their other hand. His dad was the obvious leader in his mind. They all listened while Teddy was saying something. Teddy led them into the doorway of the basement and was about to close the door when, he looked at his son and the camera.

"Hey son."

"Hey Dad. Where y'all going?"

"Down here to take care of a little business."

"Business? What kind of business?"

"The kind that's none of yours."

They all laughed as he closes the door.

"Assholes," David said then, on camera, and he says the same thing whenever he thinks of them laughing at him.

The rap music blaring from Lollypop wasn't a new thing, it was too old. Many of the other stores and folks with kiosks near Peaches complained.

David saw Oren, the security guard, moving into the store. David befriended him because Oren was the only guard that didn't fear the criminals.

"What's up, playboy?" David said.

"You know what's good. Gotta keep that music down for me."

"It's Christmas. I am just trying to get the spirit flowing."

"Just keep it down, for me."

"For you? For you, I'll do it."

David reached down and turned the knob.

"You shouldn't even be playing that," a young customer complained. "It's corny. Play some real Christmas music, like some hardcore Christmas."

David sighed. It was back to reality. "Right. You buying something?"

"I'm just looking," the kid's tone changed.

"Well keep on looking. When you buy something I'll consider your opinion."

"Buster."

The guard shook his head. "Thank you."

"Anytime. For you. And Oren?"

The guard stopped from leaving and turned to look back.

"Don't change, don't ever change."

Smiling, the guard shook his head and proceeded on his rounds.

Out from the back of the store came David's sexy boss, 23 year-old Ginata Davis. She was wearing the same powder blue work polo shirt as David, but her lanyard says manager.

Ginata hated the song and David had the damn thing blaring, on repeat. But she felt for David's loss. His dad was a good man and this was his dad's time of year; so she gave him leeway. He could have played *Bow Wow's* horrible Christmas CD and she wouldn't have complained. Besides, Ginata wants David, always has since the day she hired him. Ginata liked how he doted after her, showed her love despite the fact that she understood David was in love with his childhood sweetheart. Can't compete with that, was Ginata's thinking.

David noticed that Ginata was frowning. "Why the sad face, boss lady?"

"Where is dizzy with my lunch?" she said while moving behind the counter.

"A) I don't know. B) I don't know why you let him go for you. You know he gonna come back wrong."

Ginata sucked her teeth. She changed the subject, trying to avoid the oncoming anger. "So, what's up with the party?"

"I don't know. Adam wants to have it. I don't know about my mother, though."

Ginata nodded her head. "I hope you have it. I love that party, but I could understand how Ms. Verdie might not want to continue that tradition without her husband."

"Yeah."

"Well, let me know. I was going to bring my man."

"Oh really?"

"Don't start nothing," She checked off an item on her clipboard and moved out to the DVD section.

"I can't wait to see this mystery man that keeps us apart."

"Shut up."

On Ginata's heels, a sexy woman came to the counter. The first thing David noticed was the woman's fleshy breasts squeezing out from a too small, low cut, v-neck blouse. She had high-pressed hair and a mouth of gold teeth.

"What can I do you for?" David asked, trying to keep his eyes steady on her green eyes. Green eyes...weird he thought. They didn't seemed to fit her big golden tanned brown body, still she was attractive.

"The new Blackshear," she said softly, and she threw a blink.

"How many you want?"

"How many I want? How many you going to hook me up with?"

"I can't do that, love."

"Come on, you can do anything," she said, her hand found his on the counter and she slowly rolled her fingers over his hand. She smiled at him.

"My momma don't like me talking to pretty girls. She said y'all can't be trusted. At all."

"Your momma don't know what you'll get being nice to me."

"You can't flirt with me, though. That's my girl right there, for real."

David pointed at Ginata over at the right of the store, by the DVDs.

"That dyke? You missing it."

"Don't call my girl that. She feminine...like soft and sweet."

"Stop being lame."

"You buying or begging?"

She twisted her mouth and took her hand off his finally. "Yeah okay. But you foul."

David turned and took down the CD and scanned it into the register. "That will be sixteen dollars and four cents for you."

The sexy customer mouthed a curse.

"Now was that ladylike?"

She pulled out a thick knot of twenties and peeled off one and handed it to David. She snickered and said, "Why you so lame?"

"Sorry boo. Can I keep the change?"

"Hell nah you can't."

LaQuan Anthony entered the store with a bag and two fingers up in the peace sign.

LaQuan, 27, nearly a six-footer, was David's not too bright best friend and co-worker. They had gone to high school together and David got him a job working with him. He too is wearing the Lollypop uniform.

David had to laugh at the sight of him, "Fool, where you been?"

LaQuan watched the behind of the sexy girl that David had been dealing with as she left. He mouths an O.

"I know you ain't get her number, yo.

"Not. What I need a number of a nasty girl?"

"You stupid. Nasty girls is the best. And you don't need to be turning down numbers, for real.

"Kid, you the dumb one."

Ginata came to the counter and let out a long sigh. "What, you went home to make it?"

"Out of my business, right now."

"Where have you been? I am starving."

"Oh, so nobody cares that I was in line for a half an hour?"

"Nope," David said.

"I care. Thank You," Ginata said softly.

LaQuan smiled at David.

Then Ginata became agitated. "What the? What is this?"

"Your lunch," LaQuan frowned.

"What, I don't even know what this is."

"I was in line for a long time. I forgot what you had said you didn't want, so I got them to put everything on the side."

"Uh uh, no, look at this-"

David was dying to see what his boy done messed up now. He craned his neck to see in the bag.

LaQuan was shaking his head.

Ginata was also, and she said, "But, Quan? They put everything in one cup. Mustard, mayonnaise, ketchup, pickles, onions, peppers. Olives? Olives? That's what I didn't want."

"Oh."

She opened the sandwich. "The sandwich is just bare?"

David was laughing. "You see, I told you not to send him."

Ginata went on, "Ham? Ham? I said turkey breast."

"You said spicy ham."

"I did not. I don't even know what the hell spicy ham is."

David was laughing harder. He had to get under control; he had to ask, "What the hell is spicy ham?"

"Well, what? You don't want it?"

"No. I am not eating this mess. You a stupid little something in this world."

David bent over laughing.

LaQuan was mumbling curse words.

"Oh, you two are too much!" David said, tears in his eyes. "Oh, Lord, I ain't laugh this much since the last caper you two went on.

"Nice job messing up my lunch, moron."

"Whatever," LaQuan snapped.

"Now now. You said not to call him names, remember?"

"That was before that idiot messed up my damn lunch.

"Yo, hold up. I'm stupid because you don't know what you want? I ain't no waiter and I ain't your man."

"Then you know what, you shouldn't have offered to go to get my sandwich." She bullied passed LaQuan and toward the mall. "I am getting me something I can eat."

David laughed again. He said, "Okay. Take care." He turned to his friend, "Player, you ain't never, never ever, gonna get them panties now."

LaQuan waved a hand. "Bunk her. She stay mad. That man she brag on, he ain't hitting it right."

4

Adam Taylor didn't like rap music, or that whole Hip-Hop attitude and movement. In a nutshell, he thought all of that was crap; young people being ignorant. And he had no time for ignorance or nonsense. He was on a mission, a mission, though, whose theme he stole from a hot 90s rap song: Money Power & Respect.

That was all he wanted. He knew he could get all that from being mayor of Atlanta. A position he knew he could make a nice piece of change on the side, he didn't care about how he made the money, dirty or whatever, he just wanted to be paid, and he damn sure would take advantage of the power running the city would afford him. And respect would come easily to the son of Teddy Taylor that became mayor.

That was why this year's Christmas party was very important to Adam. He had to have it go on as usual. He was going to use the party as a fund raising tool. Play off the fact that his dad knew everybody in the state of Georgia that had money and power and they all respected his dad.

So the first move Adam made was to connect with Dan Sweeney, the most powerful congressman in Georgia. Adam had heard Sweeney so many times beg Adam's father to run for office. Adam didn't mind that Sweeney wanted a puppet for mayor.

His dad worked with him so he had to be cool, was Adam's thinking. He had blocked out the head to head confrontations his dad had with Sweeney. All Adam considered was that he had plenty to offer. He was already as respected as an active city councilman and he had that family name.

Thelma's was a high class restaurant in Buckhead, an upper class section of Atlanta. It was a place his dad frequented, and some rumored that he knew Thelma well.

It was where Adam decided to have his big meeting with the man that was about to set his career soaring. The two well dressed men finished up their meals. During their small talk while eating Sweeney stared at Adam almost seductively as he spoke.

"I miss your dad. One hell of a man. Honest and no bullshit.

"Yes, sir. He was the best, father and politician I will ever know."

"How's your mom?"

"She is as expected. She doesn't go out much, but once we get passed this first Christmas, I think she'll be cool.

"I gotta say this." Sweeney took a sip of water, "For me, Theodore was great. He was an innovator. He was a trailblazer, and the way he showed social commentary in his humorous way opened up a universe for his people to want follow him."

Theodore was arguably the biggest name in Georgia politics during the 1990s. Your father would have hated to hear this, but he would have made and excellent mayor."

"I believe that too. And, the funny thing was, he didn't like politics."

"How true, how true." Sweeney took in the look from Adam. He could feel the thoughts swirling, and the memory of how much of a hard ass Theodore Taylor had been with his high morals and low tolerance for bullshit.

Adam softened, "But he never dissuaded nor discouraged me."

"And I don't think you could be discouraged. You seem very determined."

Adam felt vindicated, understood.

Sweeney watched the busboy fill his glass with water, and when the young man moved to Adam's glass, Sweeney took his and took a sip.

"Well," Sweeney said, "needless to say he wasn't much for crawling before walking-he always had his sights set high. And I see that in you too, Councilman."

"Well, thank you Mr. Sweeney. I still feel there's no better replacement for him than you."

"And your family's support went a long way in putting me in congress. I'd like to show my appreciation by fully backing your campaign to the tune of...two point five million dollars."

Adam is a little taken aback. He sips water.

"Mr. Sweeney, I..."

"Look, Adam...with an even moderate campaign I have no doubt you can win. And a congressman is only as good as the support he has from his city and state government. We have some big bills coming down the pike and I'm going to need your full support."

"Such as?"

Sweeney wiped his mouth and replied, "An education program that makes way for federal lending to private school start-ups."

Adam considered that a second. He tried to not think like his father. What might he have planned for the money?

"But that would mean the city schools would have their share of cuts, yes indeed. You're private school educated and I'm sure you can appreciate the importance of this. It means more Ted and Adam Taylor's in the world."

"My Dad put a lot into the school system here."

"And none of that would be touched. But I think I'd only be implementing his full vision of what the system could be. A system that's more privatized where the parents have more control. It's a win, win situation."

The check was brought to the table and Adam reached to sign but Sweeney was quick to stop him. "Oh, no you don't. A hardworking Councilman is always on my dime."

"I have a few dimes myself."

"Fair enough. But you are a gentleman, so let me take care of this."

Adam smiled and he yielded.

On way out door Adam was lost in the thought of power, of running a city, of his dad being proud. He missed the congressman speaking to him.

"Excuse me?"

"Is your family still having the Christmas party?"

"Everybody assumes we are having the party, so, um, why not," he lied. "We should just have it."

Adam assured himself that lying to this white man was right. It was none of Sweeney's business that the family wasn't gung ho about the party. He became aware of his body feeling heated and the sweat on his forehead.

"You and your family are doing the right thing."

Adam took up his water and sipped. "Yeah, yes, I think we are. And it will be bigger and better."

"Hey, I have an idea. Why don't we announce the campaign donation at the Christmas party?"

"Actually, that was when I was hoping it would happen. That would be great."

"We'll be there at six and I'll bring your future in a little check book...What do you say?"

Sweeney holds out his hand to Adam. Adam hesitated at first-then...he nods.

"Then I'll see you at six."

They shook hands.

5

Patricia Taylor turned up the collar on her gray wool jacket to cover the back of her neck and pulled the front together and began buttoning it. It was hard to believe that only a week ago she'd been wearing short sleeves. It was finally winter in Georgia, She could only be grateful she didn't live up north, where blizzards had already been reported.

The December sun spilled over everything, refusing uncooperatively to warm the earth with its rays. She thought by now the weather would have warmed.

Patricia had slowed down her schedule after Thanksgiving with her sights on being available to help throw the Christmas party like her dad would have wanted. But as the date the party usually popped, she was getting nervous. Maybe they shouldn't try to keep the party alive if the man that created it was no longer gong to be a part of it.

Patricia handled her business in court that day like a fem-bot. She was working on muscle memory, not saying or doing more than it took to do things right.

She leaves the courthouse, avoiding the smiles and slight flirting the guards offer. Most days it's nice, especially coming from the older, more polished men. They knew how to slide a gesture or sly word into everyday conversation. The younger ones come right out with it, like Morris Day, "You wanna make love or what?"

"Say hello to your father for me," a sudden voice said. No hello or hi first to her.

Patricia looked in his steel blue eyes and told the white, well-dressed middle aged man, "I wish I could. He passed away in the summer."

"I am very sorry."

She felt he was; but she was already sick of people being sorry for her lost. But this man would not be the last, she felt, to not know a man as well-known as her dad was no longer available to take distant hellos.

The day had already been a long one. When dawn arrived, Patricia found herself lying awake, reflecting on all that had happened.

Setting her only appointment of the day late in the afternoon afforded her the opportunity to be lazy most of the morning after working out. But also she had found herself with too much time to think. She was worried about the party happening and half her mind was a bit nervous about the man in her life.

Maybe it was her father's death catching up to her. Maybe it was the fact that she was going to be thirty with little to show for all her years.

She was alone in the quiet office she had leased and furnished with the money her dad left her. Her paralegal, Connie, was out shopping, a day off. The small office has one other lawyer, her friend from law school who was also a struggling attorney, and her paralegal. The Taylor Law firm was struggling. Her consigliore was gone. Who could she run to with questions and for advice? She was dating a good lawyer but she was not ready for Marc Jacobs to see her weaknesses.

Teddy had prepared Patricia well for the world of grown-ups and she was bright and self-dependant. But what Teddy couldn't do was prepare her for the loneliness of life without him. She very much loved to be around her brothers and her mother, but Teddy had a way to comfort, please, and entertain any soul, especially a soul he loved. And Teddy couldn't explain very well that Atlanta could be a tough spot for single women.

Her cell phone chimed a *50 Cent* rap song. She loved that shot-up man's chest, not his voice. She prayed it wasn't Marc because damn how would he know she was thinking about him. He would take that as a sign they belonged together. It was her older brother, she saw from the caller ID.

"It's on," was all Adam said.

Patricia went numb. She steered her car by memory with traffic, turning right heading for the interstate.

Adam went on, "This is big. Bigger than any party dad ever gave."

"Why you say that, that's not right to say or think."

"Stop your tripping. I love dad, and all he accomplished with his party. I am just taking it to the next level."

"Well, Dave is right, you sound selfish about this."

"Please with that. I am just trying to keep the tradition alive until momma is ready to take it over, next year hopefully."

Patricia sighed.

Cars, SUVs, and pickup trucks stretched in five lanes as far as the eyes could see from downtown Atlanta's bending highway, with brake lights that formed dotted red lines. Patricia put the convertible Mercedes in park and leaned her head against the cream head rest. The night air blew cool and blessedly free of humidity. The sky deepened to a rich sapphire, the stars set to come out through the dusk.

"You there? Tricia?"

"I hear you."

"Well, you aren't saying anything?"

"What do you want me to say? We're doing it, we're doing it. That's that."

"No, come on now. You can't be like that when we meet with Momma in the morning."

"We meeting with momma in the morning?" she said suddenly annoyed.

"Yes, hello? What are you doing? You driving? Why you not listening? We gotta have the meeting tomorrow and get this going."

She sighed. "Fine. You know, shit, I ain't got nothing to do in my life."

"This party is important for everybody."

She pictured her mother smiling. If this made her happy for a little while it would be worth it. "You right, you right." She said.

"Okay then. Let's do this. Let's get in the spirit. I need you to call your loser brother and tell him it's on and be ready for this meeting in the morning. I am gonna call Momma."

"Right."

6

Patricia flipped the phone closed and continued to drive, the traffic picking up, she moved out onto Interstate 20.

A little more than a half an hour later she pulled into an exclusive sub-division of expensive homes. She drove around back where there were still a gang of trees and wooded area and parked in a driveway. She stood out of her ride, and was greeted by the smell of people cooking out.

She was at Marc Jacob's crib, her home away from home since her dad died. Marc was five years older than Patricia's twenty-eight, and he stood over her, with dark hair, dark eyes, and eye lashes too thick to be wasted on a man. She was wildly attracted to him from the moment their eyes met at the courthouse. She knew, not only by his fly suit, but his demeanor that he was a lawyer, or someone important, and surely not a defendant. Her stroll was too composed, no bright-eyed look.

Marc understood the power his looks had but he wasn't conceited. Instead he was always so cool, and he was an overconfident pain in the ass when it came to his work as an attorney, which she liked in a man.

Marc was so much like her father. He was a born leader, a take-charge kind of man who made instant decisions and issued orders, expecting them to be obeyed. The time she had spent with him had taught her so much about him, certainly enough to make her fall head over heels in love.

She hadn't dated for nearly a year when they met and he was the first man to make her feel tempted to be alone with.

There was no denying the chemistry between them, and while she might just have wanted a one-night affair to quench her desires, he craved something far more long-term with her. Over the ensuing months he'd come to realize that she was the kind of woman he'd been searching years to find. She was genuinely smart and caring, inherently sensual, and she didn't have one eye on being his wife and the other eye on his bank account and all that his money might be able to buy her.

But she now realized she had barely scratched the surface. There were still volumes to learn, depths to investigate and understand. But in what capacity was she going to explore this man.

Marc was going to let her do it her way, she was sure. He just wanted to be with her, he told her. In his actions, he proved that he loved her independence, assertiveness, competitive, and combative, but every once in awhile he knew she would lean on him; and he was always there, no question.

After a month of fooling around, movies, home dinners that were merely preludes to sex, and no serious dates or talks, he told her he loved being with her.

They woke up together one morning and his gaze locked onto her eyes. "I'm afraid I am falling in love with you," he said.

"Do you know what love is?" Patricia asked softly.

"Yes, I do. I messed with the words and been hurt by the feeling enough to say yes I do know what love is."

Marc Jacob heard the car come to a halt. He came through the house to greet his lady. He opened the door to find her there.

"Hey," Patricia said softly.

"Hey you," Marc smiled. Come on in."

He had the grill out back fired up and was prepping the meat and veggies like a New York chef. She had to admire that she was coming to his house after a long day and he was thoughtful enough to make dinner.

Marc moved toward the living room. Marc caught her hand and pulled her beneath the mistletoe. He kissed her gently and after a brief hesitation she kissed him back.

"This is how you get free kisses in your own house?"

"Nope. I put that up just for you. So I can get you to kiss more than that little bit you be giving."

"No. Really now?"

"True.

"Maybe you are just lip greedy."

He wrapped his arms around her and kissed her face with soft pecks, from cheek to cheek, stopping at her lips to nibble. She surrendered, wrapping her arms around his neck. It hit her suddenly, she wanted him, and she had been turned on that fast.

She took hold of his manhood under his jeans. "I want some of this."

He grinned, "I guess so. You holding it pretty tightly. But let me remind you, I ain't with quickies."

"Do like you do."

She had to pant when he swiped her off her feet and carried her up to his room. When he laid her down on the bed he stood tall and began undressing. "I am hungry, the grill is going, today, just this once, I have to do you in under an hour."

"Shut up. You wasting time."

A half an hour later, Patricia came back down stairs wearing his robe.

"God, I love this house.

"Me too. You acting like you haven't been here before."

"Still, it's nice and big and cozy. You doing pretty nicely for yourself."

"Why thank you. Your cribo is pretty nice too."

"Thanks. But I wouldn't have the house had my dad not passed away."

She steals a slice of green pepper off the grill. She fought the searing with her fingers and then by blowing while chewing.

"You would have had any house you wanted. You got it going on."

"Maybe in a decade," she said, chewing. "The food smells good."

"Grab the salad dressing out of the fridge."

"Sure," she said, but she felt funny. Why was he so comfortable with her? He didn't say please, as if they were an old married couple. Was it because he liked her? Because they had slept together more than 20 times in the two months they knew each other?

Plate in hand, Marc gets the steaks. He returns to find Tricia setting their plates.

"Steaks in the middle of the week, you living nice, Mr. Jacobs."

"Money make a Black be like that. How did everything go at court?" Marc asked, as he plopped down beside her.

"Sweet. Like it was supposed to."

"It's nearing time for the party."

Patricia nodded. She knew he was asking, just like everybody else, he wanted to know if the party was on.

"I only met your dad once, but I liked him."

"I miss him."

"I bet you do. He was cool. How's your mom?"

"She's good, thanks. She should be better now that we have decided to throw the party."

"Oh, cool. That would be good for her. Great." Marc sat, "so you and your brothers came to an agreement?"

"Something like that."

"You and your brothers are doing the right thing."

"I think so. I hope so," Adam almost choked, almost in tears. "I gotta call David."

Marc watched her go into the house. He admired her slim, shapely body as much as the strength she right then didn't know she possessed. She'll be okay, he thought, and he vowed to help her get through it.

Patricia suddenly remembered she had to call David and let him know the great news.

"I gotta call Dave," she sighed annoyingly.

Marc nodded.

She stepped away from Marc and felt his eyes follow her. She snuck a look to see his eyes were pleading, caring. Shit, he cares all the time, she thought.

"Baby sister."

"What you doing, robbing our people with the high ass prices?" She joked. Since they were little, David's voice, his joyful way of conversing had always put Tricia at ease.

"That's how we do it. What's cracking?"

"We are definitely doing this. The party is on. I just talked to Adam. He wants to do it."

"Really now?"

"Yeah we coming over tomorrow to discuss the details. He is planning to do most of it himself."

"Yeah, he thinks it will make him mayor to have control of the party. He act like I don't see what's going down. It don't matter though."

"What about momma?"

"Oh. I don't know. She is still fighting the depression. So me, I think she needs the big party atmosphere, for real."

"Me too," she sighed. "I gotta go. I am at Marc's."

"Whoa, Mr. Marcus. Tell him I said hi."

"Stop calling him that. He gets geeked-up like he got it like the real Mr. Marcus."

"He better not have it like no porn star. Not with my sister."

"Shut up. See you."

David put his cell in his pocket and made the announcement.

"Yes! Yes! Yes!" LaQuan jumped in the air and pumped his fists.

"Okay now buy a toothbrush."

Ginata laughed. She came closer to David from the aisles. "Well, I was hoping for this." David didn't get it, despite the sparkle in her eyes. "I gotta make a call," she took her tiny pink phone out and dialed a number.

"And who are you calling?"

She sensed a pang of jealousy and liked it.

"I am not going alone this year. I am going to have me a date. Last year I couldn't even get a look, let alone a dance, from you."

"Really now?"

"Yes, you were all over that kissing cousin of yours."

"Please."

LaQuan squealed.

7

Moments later another sign that this just might be a nice holiday for David came through the door of the store. The tall, voluptuous Yvette Paulding walked in and David lit up like a Christmas tree at night.

"There's my lady."

Yvette couldn't stop a blush from taking over her grin. How beautiful he made her feel, how utterly lovely. He conveyed with a look, with a touch, how special he found her.

"Damn. That smile."

"Hey."

"Hey back at ya. How you doing?"

"Okay. I came by to see if you guys are going to have the party."

"Seems that way. If not, we can do a little something, go out."

Yvette shook her head slowly. "Well, I am not really feeling the holidays. I was going to say that I might just stay home."

"You not feeling it? You will. I got you a gift."

"Thank you. But you didn't have to do that. That's not what I mean. I rather be alone for Christmas."

"No not that. That's not the answer. Don't do that."

She smiled again although she sure didn't feel like smiling. He was doing that to her. "I'm just..."

David came from behind the counter. "What's up? I mean, we all kinda bummed out about Christmas, but we having the party. I thought you'd be excited."

Yvette looked away. She was nervous and so trying not to show it. Her eyes caught on a woman with a tiny baby in her arms and a toddler at her feet. She pushed her thoughts from the negative.

"What's going on Yvette?"

She smiled, "You know me too well, don't you?"

"Shit, you been my girl ten years and change. You snatched my virginity. I know you."

She laughed. "You took mine, tell it real."

"Well, we did it together. Nasty like."

"You so silly."

"But what's going down? Since Thanksgiving you been acting kind of ghost. I am feeling a lot like you dropping me like LL dropped Bobcat Earl."

"I been busy. I got my place. You know, my mother is tripping. My dad is out of town a lot. It's just been crazy."

"But damn, you can call your man though."

"you right, you right. I was thinking you have a lot going on with your mother."

"I do. But we got history. You can come over anytime."

"Yeah, you slick. I come over there you are not trying to talk."

"Well, that's bound to happen. But now you talking about you not coming to the party?"

"I don't know. I may stop in for a second. I am just not feeling the holidays."

David turned serious. "Look, listen," David said, "just come to chill for a little while. Get your gift, have a drink, something to eat and I'll get you home at a decent hour."

Yvette considered the offer. Fun was something David could share with no effort, and that was something she would always love about him.

David went on, "No stress. Just think about it. I'd like for you to be there, and you know moms would, but if you not feeling it, don't force it."

"Okay."

David took her hand. They exchange glances. Yvette looks away. She moves away. "I gotta go."

"Think about it. Call me."

"Okay. Okay. I will."

"I hope so."

She left with a smile, disappearing out the store toward the food court.

LaQuan came up on David out of nowhere.

"You nasty, playboy. Banging a cousin like that."

David frowned and crumbled his face in a grimace at LaQuan.

"Brush your teeth. I can smell the chitlings you ate Thanksgiving, fool."

"For real? Nah you can't."

David noticed Ginata cut her eyes away when he looked at her. He thought she was doing it about LaQuan but the look on her face was something else. She had been watching David and Yvette's conversation and she despised his love for her because she could see the big girl just wasn't feeling the same way.

When he offered that love to her, Ginata was thinking, she was going to enjoy it and reciprocate. And the man was going to be her husband.

8

Verdie waited up for David to come home from work.

She wasn't sure what she would say to him. They were going to have the party, with or without her consent. She had to say what was on her mind, though.

She was trying to deal. Telling herself this was the season of goodwill. The time for peace on earth and strong family unity, and, of course, the time for Theodore Taylor's effing Christmas party.

Verdie had the photo albums out. They were thick, big ones that she and Teddy had gotten especially for the Christmas party photos. The pages were filled with hundred of shots taken through the years. One thing she noticed that night that she hadn't ever noticed: there weren't enough pictures of her husband.

David came in with very little noise, as was his habit living with his 77 year-old grandmother and his sad mother. He came in the kitchen hoping to find his mother willing to talk. He saw the plate on the stove covered by a napkin. At first he felt bad that he didn't remember his mother was going to cook, but she hadn't. it wasn't her norm to cook lately. Then he felt bad that he had eaten *Wendy's* with LaQuan.

"I made you some dinner."

"Thanks, Momma. I ate already though," he had his voice soft to meet her low decibel. "Me and Quan grabbed a little something something."

"It's okay."

"Yeah, you know I'ma eat it eventually."

"So I see y'all are going to do this?"

"Yeah, Ma."

She had a smile on her face but nothing in her demeanor told a story of her being happy.

"You remember your cousin Gerard?"

Of course he did. They were tight. Gerard got killed by his girlfriend's ex four years before Teddy passed. It was sad, G's mom never got over it.

"He came to the Christmas party every year with a six pack of beer for himself."

David grinned and shook his head at the memory of G sitting on the couch with the beer on the floor at his feet.

"And then he has the nerve to say he don't like to come empty handed."

"Ma, he didn't know any better. And I bet you this, ours was the only party he went all year. People need this party."

"You mean your brother needs this party."

"We all do. You too."

Verdie shook her head. "I do not need a party. Your father was more than a party."

"Right, right. He was. But this was his main event. And ain't nobody not have a good time. It's more than a Christmas party. It's like an end of the year get together."

"Is Rev. Penny coming?"

"Uh uh. I don't think so. The only crooks Adam invited are white."

Verdie chuckled.

"I take that back. The Rev. knows when and where. He'll be there to eat some home cooking."

"I am not cooking," Verdie said.

"For real? Come on now?"

"It wasn't my idea."

"Oh."

"No," she became agitated, "your brother called and told me he don't need me to cook."

"He said it like that?"

"No," her voice softened. "He said I need a rest, that he can take care of it. He just needs this party for his gains."

"We all need this, momma. All of us. You too."

"Now don't go telling me what I need. My husband started all this. This was his. You three think you can just, just take over."

"No, Momma. Where you get that from?" He was realizing his mother's hurt had set in and was turning her bitter.

"Well, I mean, what does it matter how I feel since y'all done made up your minds?"

"Momma; listen, please, okay? Just have a good time, for me, for us. Whatever Adam's reason is, whatever, I feel like we should have the party. But I want to be happy about it."

"I don't know what I want."

9

Adam Taylor married the leggy, breathtaking Mardessa Coleman. She was fine, chocolate, tall sister. She was as sexy as she was smart. She called her persona that of a Spelman woman.

It was a big wedding, over 500 guests. The two families though, haven't been a good mix since. The women in Adam's life, his mother, sister, grandmother and auntie BeBe thought Mardessa was unfriendly. What bothered them was the way she too often spoke about wanting a lighter complexion.

Mardessa called them clannish. Her family thought Adam was selfish and single-minded. All he wanted, the Coleman's believed, was to be mayor, with their attractive relation on his arm, smoothing his image.

Adam didn't give a damn either way. They were right; all he cared about was being mayor. Marrying Mardessa was different prize. He loved her, no doubt, but his eyes were on the prize.

Adam called his wife at her gig, "Baby we going out to celebrate."

Adam loved eating out as much as he loved his dainty wife. And Mardessa really liked his penchant for dining in the finest, fanciest Atlanta restaurants. The night it was decided there would be a Christmas party; they went to her favorite spot, an expensive seafood restaurant in the elite Buckhead section of Atlanta.

Once they placed their orders, Mardessa got the 10-pound lobster, with sautéed shrimps on the side, and Adam got the surf & turf, Adam started right in excitedly about the party.

"This is it. All I was working for is coming together."

"What did your mother say?" Mardessa asked, taking a sip of her wine as soon as the waiter finished pouring.

Adam, a great talker paused. Mardessa checked his face.

"She's with it."

"Is she?"

"We'll take care of it. She won't have to lift a finger. It's my brother I am worried about. David just doesn't get it."

"Hmmm."

"He has gone through Dad's money. We got our inheritance in September and he's broke living with our mother."

"What the hell did he do with it?"

"Who knows? Bought X Box games and crap like that; like he's 12 years old or something."

"Today at work..."

"He didn't even get a place to stay at least. Only giving forty dollars. I could kick his ass."

"Maybe that is all he has?"

"And maybe I don't believe that. Anyway, like it matters? We got this. This is my party now. And it will be a classy affair."

Their food arrived.

10

It snowed the morning Verdie Taylor's grown children were going to decide for definite whether or not to go on with plans for the Christmas Party her husband made famous.

The snow came down in light, puffy feathery flakes. It was a picturesque despite the clouds. But to Verdie, it was just another dull and overcast day dawning in Georgia.

The weather didn't matter to Verdie. It matched her spirits. All she saw was another day in Atlanta dawning, dull and overcast. She did consider, though, that snow at Christmas was not a good thing in Atlanta, despite the coming of Christmas. Up north it would have been for the kids but in Georgia, she considered, it was going to be hell on traffic and the grocery stores were going to be packed with folks buying milk, water and batteries.

As the weeks had passed from Thanksgiving, she had been unhappy before, but rarely had she felt this listlessness, this apathy toward what life had to offer. Now it was December, again. This used to be her favorite time of the year, and now she dreaded Christmas, a thought she couldn't have dreamed less than a year ago. But now, her eyes as lifeless as the leaves she stared at, Verdie grinned with memory.

These days she enjoyed staying in bed but at night if she'd sleep twenty minutes it was a lot. She hadn't slept well since...since August. Since he stormed out angry and never came back to her; since the last time her husband was in the bed with her, to hold her to make her feel like a loved woman.

The temperature rose, and by the time Verdie decided to get out of the bed, all the white snow had turned to water.

Mindlessly she pushed herself up out of the bed and went to the tall window facing the street. She moved the curtains and looked for normalcy. Although she was so sad, she still had to look and see people living their lives. Across the street, there he was, Rolando Gomez, a police officer, getting into his new Hummer, on his way to work as he did at six every morning. His wife was up, Verdie was sure, getting their two girls ready for school. They will be leaving the house in about an hour or so, they were always late.

Next to the Gomez's was Joe Mann and his live-in girlfriend...and there she came out, on cue as Verdie moved her eyes from the departing Hummer, a broke version of Beyonce, she was all legs and hair. Everybody else in the block, all working folks of different ages, will be up and out by nine-thirty, all working in different parts of greater Atlanta.

When the action died down for a moment, and the street quieted, the trees that lined the sidewalk dropped, the leaves were drained of life.

She was determined not to sink into gloom. She got up from the window. She'd been up for hours, yet she hadn't eaten a thing. Food. That was the answer, Verdie assured herself.

At 54, and Sleep or no sleep, she was still attractive despite the toll the sadness of losing her husband.

Verdie was an Atlanta girl. Teddy fell for her while he was in the south gaining knowledge; he was attending Morehouse from Chicago. Southern curves. That's what he called her. She was a church girl, quiet, always had her legs showing and was never at the cool parties or places around town.

The first time he saw his wife he knew he loved her for life. And on their second date a feeling swept over him, an eager hunger that made him feel surprisingly alive. He pulled her close and kissed her. She moaned and wrapped herself around him, kissing back eagerly.

"I like you, Verdie," he told her.

"I like you too, Teddy."

Teddy's gaze shifted, but never left her face. She liked that.

Verdie's words became deeper, sharper, and hotter. "How do you like me?"

His response was, "In every way. In the way a man loves a woman. In the way a husband is devoted to his wife. And that is not explaining it all because I can't."

Verdie smiled at the memory.

But by the time she waddled down to the kitchen on aching feet, her dogs were hurting from lack of use, she didn't want to eat. No, Verdie protested silently, she didn't want food, she wanted Teddy.

Teddy.

The food forgotten, Verdie closed her eyes, filling her mind with an image of him. So many sad thoughts, he had passed away without ever seeing his grandchildren. With his free spirit, his storytelling skills, he would have made an excellent grandfather.

She put on a pot of water to have tea instead. She stood at the stove until the pot whistled.

11

Clutching the New York City mug Patricia had brought back from one of her many trips, Verdie gulped at the warm liquid in a futile attempt to quench the flames of sorrow locking her senses into depression. Observing her trembling fingers as if they belonged to someone else, she felt a sinking feeling in her stomach.

With the silent cry ringing in her mind, Verdie exerted every ounce of will power she possessed in an effort to appear coolly composed as she raised her eyes.

Raising the cup to her lips, Verdie's eyes closed,

Although she couldn't get herself motivated to do those things this year without her husband, she now remembers a good past, filled with marvelous memories of great times and great people at the parties.

And she'd like to keep it that way...just the memories. No new ones, no party without her husband. She knew then that she had to tell her children not to have the party.

She gulped back a sob along with the tepid brew. Would the nightmare memories never end? Would the part of remembrance never subside?

Her mother snapped her conscious back to today.

"What, you on memory lane, dream girl?" her mother said.

"Morning, momma."

"I want some of that tea. No flavor."

"Yes, ma'am." Verdie got her out a mug. "You sleep well?"

"Like a crook before a big heist. I kept getting up to use the bathroom. I didn't know rum makes you pee. Now I know."

Verdie smiled. Gently blowing on her tea, she studied her mother over the rim of her cup as she settled into a spot at the table.

Where would she have been without Pauline Peters, the mother of the year, this year? Her mom moved in and actually brought sunshine to the house. She eased Verdie with stories and busy talk. And she was always positive, even when she was nagging.

"Momma you okay? You want me to cut on a light?"

"I'm fine. There's plenty of sunlight coming in. It's snowing. You remember the last time it snow. Crazy Teddy went out and bought a damn snowblower from a crackhead."

Verdie's mind was a clogged vacuum cleaner bag that needed emptying. "I don't even remember," she said.

"It was like, 1985. And Teddy actually thought he was going to do some business with that thing. He was going to hire the neighborhood kids to clean the sidewalks and driveways all over the damn city."

Verdie shook her head.

"And you know what happened, don't you? The next day it was 45 damn degrees. All the damn snow melted.'

Verdie laughed.

Damn it, Momma. You did it again!

Verdie heard the cars pull up to the house. She moved to the window that looked out over the end of the driveway and saw her daughter's Mercedes as it stopped. She watched as her oldest walked over and hugs her only daughter hello.

Verdie smiled.

She took a second to look around and her smile became relaxed at the sight of the houses around hers all decorated for Christmas. Multi-colored lights were strung everywhere. Lit icicles from eves of houses. Plastic Santas, some complete with sleigh and reindeer, were either perched on rooftops or on green lawns.

Right then, all she consider was the legacy her husband left behind: three bright children with bright futures. In his death the three of them had used their inheritance wisely, she thought.

Her children came in and kissed their momma hello.

"My God," Granny clutched the top of her housecoat.

"What?" Patricia asked worried.

"What is it, momma," Verdie chimed in.

"That boy looks just like his daddy. Scary." She got up. "Excuse me. He done scared the piss loose in me."

"Oh, Lord," Verdie laughed. "All my children are here."

"Yeah, where's the bum?"

Verdie frowned, "Don't call your brother a bum."

Sis fixed herself a mug of coffee.

"Explain to me how he can be happy working in a mall. That ain't what daddy had in mind."

Patricia said, "If you stop being mad at him you'd see he was happy. And you are not."

"That's the problem. He's happy living off you and having no responsibilities.

"He is not living off me."

"Well, where is happy boy?"

"In his room. He worked late yesterday."

"I'ma go wake him up."

"Probably still in his Sponge Bob one-piece pajamas playing on his X Box and smoking weed."

"Adam, now."

Adam bullied into his little brother's room with Patricia on his heels, no knock. They found David asleep with his mouth open and hands under the covers.

"Look at this room," Adam winced. "Jesus. What, is he 15?"

The cluttered room had clothes everywhere, a bowl and spoon on one nightstand, empty fast food wrappers on the other. His X Box was still on, a game on pause. A man held a gun to another man's head, waiting for David to give the order, push the button, so he could kill the guy.

Adam moved in, kicking clothes out of his way to the bed. "Get your hand out of your panties and get up, you got company."

David spun slowly, too much of his body parts showed; Patricia grimaced.

"What, your girl is here already?" David said groggily.

"What, you sleep to noon?"

"That's why God created seven days, one to rest, playboy." David turned his back to his siblings and cuddled his pillow, with the crack of his buttocks showing. "Good morning, counselor."

Patricia nodded, still holding her nose, she said, "Ill, okay, crack kills."

"And good morning, congressman."

"Asshole. Stop calling me that."

With his back still to them he said, "Congress, city council. Orange, tangerines. Same thing."

Patricia said, "Sunday is the seventh day, the day of rest. Open a Bible some Dave, you heathen."

"Sunday is the first day of the week," scratching his butt under the covers.

"Yes, a mall employee telling me what's right." Patricia said.

"I try," David said.

Patricia shook her head, "It smells in here. Like nasty, last week funk is still around."

David pulled the covers over his behind.

"Why Momma doesn't have a tree up?"

"Why you think? We always wait until the day of the party." He pulled his blanket over his head. "Stop ripping off your clients and pay some attention to fam."

"Shut up, smelly."

Adam kicked the bed, "Come on and get up. We can finish this mature argument in the kitchen, Mom is in there. Wash your behind and put some clothes on, we'll meet in the kitchen."

"And I love you too."

12

Nearly twenty minutes later, David came into the kitchen with a whoosh.

"Mom, baby! The smells..." he plants a kiss on her forehead. "this is what a man is supposed to wake up to."

Verdie smiled.

"What is that supposed to mean?" his sister demanded to know.

"Exactly what I said. When you find you a man, you'll know."

"Oh, you got jokes, stinky poo? Why can't you make your own breakfast?"

"Ya dippin', counselor."

Verdie rose off her chair and prepared her youngest his plate. She said, "Anybody else want breakfast?"

"No thanks, momma," Patricia said. "I just want some juice."

"Sit," Verdie said, "I'll get it."

"Yes, sit, my dear. Momma, get her some of the good orange juice, from my stash. It's on me, dear sister."

"Shut up, stinky."

"Real mature."

Adam cut in angrily, "You know what, Bummy D? We ate breakfast at our own places, in our own kitchens."

"Fool, please. And? Like these are not my Eggos and this ain't my kitchen? You better go on before you get punched on."

Adam rolled his eyes.

David said, "Listen, on the real, if we are going to do this, then we need to just ask everybody to bring something."

"You crazy? Dad wasn't living like that."

"Look, I mean, this ain't dad's party anymore. I love him, he started this, true that. But he isn't here, and then of course it changes everything. He would go broke feeding all those people. It was fun and it was nice, but like you just said, we not living like he was. We don't have his extra income or his shortcuts to deal with the cost of throwing that type of party."

"No thanks. Nice speech. We keeping it the same as always.

"He makes sense though," Patricia said.

David said, "Adam wants to turn this into a Black Tie affair."

"And you want it to be a pork and beer affair," Adam said angrily.

"Funny."

"There will be none of them alley bats you screwing at my party."

"Your party?" Patricia barked.

Verdie looked up, as displeased with her son's choice of words as her only daughter.

Their grandmother, chewing bacon as best she can without her teeth in, began to clap her hands slowly. When she had their attention, she said, "And the arguing? That makes the party better, the same or worse?"

No one spoke for a moment. In that time no eyes met.

Adam spoke first, "We should just have the party like it was. Period."

David had his mouth full of food and tried to speak his peace, "You know, they might all think it's stereotypical because it happens often, might that be the reason?"

"What?" Patricia said. "What did you say?"

Verdie and Grandmomma frowned, trying to understand.

Adam waved, "Don't shine your ignorance my way."

"Huh?"

"Exactly."

"I am saying either way we almost have to do this, have the party. Us, all together. The people right here in this room. Daddy never wanted help, he handled it all. So now, I'm just saying, it's on us."

When he finished talking, he looked to his mother for her reaction and she didn't look up or say a thing.

"Ah, hello, isn't that what I have been saying?" Adam said.

"No! You want it to be a white thing."

"I never said that!"

"Who you yelling at?"

"Ain't nobody yelling!"

"Come on. My food ain't going down right 'cause you yelling."

"Shut up. You sound gay with that."

"Gay, look what you wearing? You ain't buy that shirt in no men's department."

"How you know? You going by the men's department in Wal-Mart then no, they don't have this Egyptian cotton there."

Grandmomma snickered, "Oh, now you *Superfly*?"

"You mean *Shaft*. He stole that line from the movie. He ain't got nothing but Mississippi cotton on his ashy elbows."

"That's right, *Shaft*. Oh yes. Peoples. A pretty man, almost bald. I like that."

Patricia laughed.

"And alley bats? I'll have you know that sometimes that is the best tasting bat there is."

"Okay, now," Verdie frowned.

Patricia shook her head away from the image of her brother with some ghetto girl. "Anyway," she said, "Momma, have you heard from Daddy's side? Are they coming to the party?"

Verdie caught Adam's glare and then noticed suddenly all eyes were on her. That was a question she feared would come up. For months she had done a good job of avoiding speaking about her husband's family and their anger toward her for not having the kind of funeral they so wanted for him.

She simply said, "No, and I don't expect to hear from them or see them."

"They still mad?" Patricia asked.

"So what they not coming," David said angered. "For real though, bunk them."

"What," Patricia pressed, "are they still mad because they wanted to control the funeral? That's our father."

Verdie nodded and breathed out the word, "Probably."

"Like I so eloquently said, bunk them," David added in her defense.

"Shut up with the eloquent," Adam waved. "You wouldn't know eloquent if it kissed you on your crusty lips."

David blew his brother a kiss.

Adam went on, "They are his family, his brothers, his mother, his sisters. They had a right to want a say so."

David waved him off. "Whatever. You tripping." Then he lowered his voice sweetly and said, "Momma, my *Eggos* ain't burning, is they?"

"No, baby."

"Thank you, Momma. I trust you. For real."

Patricia was shaking her head, "I can't believe they are still upset. I called Grandma and she was all short on the phone."

"That's because she ain't never really learned how to use the phone...modern technology and mess."

Verdie put his waffles in front of David, "David, okay now," she said and then gave him a light one-handed shove.

"Sorry, Momma. And momma, this ain't enough, for real. I am a working man."

Verdie drops two more waffles and leans her back against the counter with her arms folded. She doesn't want to say anything but she wanted to hear her children discuss her in-laws.

Adam exhaled teeth in disgust. "When I die, and God forbid something happens to me-"

"You mean like one of your constituents beats you to death?" David quipped.

"-y'all will not let my wife alone. Y'all would want to be in the middle."

"That's because she ain't gonna wanna do nothing with your cold dead butt from all them years of you getting on her nerves."

"This is getting ridiculous now," Verdie spoke up. "Your wife is your life partner. We are your family. And just like in this case, your wife will do as I did; she will abide by your wishes. Now that is that."

"Uh, zing," David exclaimed.

"So they not coming to the party?" Patricia asked. Her arms were extended out as if to ask why.

"Uh, is this conversation moving too fast for you, sis?"

Patricia added, "That's not right. They are family. They need to be here. They were here every year."

Verdie shrugged, "Things change."

"We'll be alright," David said.

Adam huffed, "What? I am calling them. They need to be here." He looked to her mother for agreement.

The *Eggos* pop up just as Verdie moves out of the kitchen.

"Momma," Patricia groaned. "Adam? You made momma cry over them?"

Adam shook his head.

They could hear their mother slam herself into her bedroom.

"Asshole," David said as he got up to get his waffles.

"How the hell do y'all get that idea? You the one, Trish. Why did you bring them up?"

"But you the one that went all there, *they gotta be there*, and all that. Why you kissing up to them? They can't vote for you, most of them are felons.

"I am getting the family together."

"Like they really family?" David said, his mouth full again. "Anytime we needed something or even when Mom was sick or something, where were they? Then when he passed, they wanted to control the damn funeral, like they all religious and shit."

Patricia added, "Once a year, eating free? That doesn't count as family.

"Must I say the F word again? Funk them."

Adam said, "I ain't letting this family fall apart. No way. Dad brought everybody together, all that love we shared, even if for just one damned day.

"Nice. Maybe they'll thank you."

Patricia bolted out of the kitchen.

"You see?" Ddavid said to Adam. "You pissing off everybody in the morning time."

Adam sighed hard. "Y'all just don't get it. What do you think daddy started this for? To end in a huff, to just end with nobody talking anymore?"

"You got a point though, on the real. But momma being happy is more important, this year. I mean, why can't we just miss a year. Come back next year strong?"

"We need it this year."

"You need it this year."

"Momma needs it too, she just don't know, she can't feel it right now."

David took in more food, chewing and considering what his brother was saying. Their mother surely needed happiness back in her life. Staring at the tiny television on the countertop, he took in account the fact that he hadn't seen his mother laugh in a very long time.

"You know what?" David finally said, "You right, though. You right. I think she do need this. At least she needs to get that spirit back. Man I don't think I have seen momma laugh since before daddy died. She needs this. Everybody here."

"That's what I am talking about, that's all I am trying to say."

"Just let me talk to her."

"We have to do this."

"Stop saying we. I'll talk to her."

"What you going to do?"

"What am I going to do? I told you I'll talk to her."

"No I mean for the party."

"What man? You got me down with the party, ain't that enough? Let me eat my breakfast."

Adam cursed. "No, I mean what are you chipping in?"

David took a sip of his OJ. "I got forty on that."

"Forty dollars? You living here rent free!"

David had taken in another mouthful. He shifted the food, and put his hand up to block his mouth. "Don't count my money, dude. That's rude."

Adam looks disgusted. "You are a bum."

"But your momma loves me though."

13

Patricia held her breath, looking at her mother's bedroom door as if it had writing on it.

She cleared her mind, making sure she was open for whatever her mother might want to say, before she tapped softly on the door. There was no answer.

Her mind zipped back through the millions of times she had slammed herself into her bedroom in tears over something her brothers had done, damn David burning Barbie's hair! Or something a boy had done, effing Paul dumping her before the senior prom because Ayanna was giving out. In all those times Verdie knocked first, and then came in. And within an hour Patricia was okay about life again.

Patricia knocked again and turned the knob and came in. She found her mother in tears on her bed. Patricia didn't know what to say or do once she was in there. The sight knocked her thoughts loose. She sat on the bed and draped her arm around her mom.

"Do you know why I had your father cremated?" Verdie said after a long silence.

Patricia shook her head; forced to look at the urn that she hadn't set eyes on in months. She softly said, "Momma, I'm telling you, as much as you loved that man. I wouldn't have had a problem if you kept him in a shoe box at the back of your closet. It's your business, not for anyone else to judge."

"No. But do you know why?"

"I'm saying, that was your man first. You ain't gotta explain."

Verdie sobbed into her daughter's chest.

"Momma, it's alright. I love you. We all do, and that is what matters."

"Your daddy wanted to be cremated. "

Patricia could see him saying that. He was never one to want to be a burden. He would want them to spend the money on getting all his friends drunk at a big party instead of giving it to a funeral home.

"Look, Ma, it's not about the funeral, you know that. They think they got a raw deal. They think they didn't get their fair share. They think more money was involved. But so what?"

Verdie shook her head. "I loved that man with my whole soul. Everything I had."

Patricia lost it, she choked and the crying just came.

Verdie kissed her and continued because she had to get it out, had to say it, "He did so much for me, supportive. It was his wish. And I wanted to grant his dying wish. He was a good man. God, I miss him."

Patricia gave off a sobbing sigh. She wiped her eyes. "We all do."

"There was nothing your father hated more than to see his boys fight and not speak. He was so proud to have three kids and so ashamed he couldn't make y'all friends."

"We are going to be okay," Patricia thought to say. "We are individuals, he taught us to be. This, you know, I think this party is something we need. It's going to help."

"I surely pray it does."

Patricia rejoined her brothers in the kitchen.

"How's momma?" David asked.

"Hurting."

Adam shook his head and sighed.

"I am with her," Patricia said, "I don't think we should have this party."

"So what, you going to change your mind every time the wind blows in a different direction?"

"What I am not going to do is let you bully me and mommy into backing you on some power move."

Adam got upset. "What, you think that is all this is? Is that what you think?"

David put his plate in the sink. "I am here with momma. I understand all she is saying and feeling right now. But let me tell, she needs this party. She needs to see all of them folk that come every year. She needs the hugs and the kisses and the attention."

Patricia could see it.

Adam sighed, "Let's do this. Let's just get it done, that's all I am saying."

David scoffed and waved, "That ain't all you saying, but yeah, let's do this."

"And you?" Adam looked at his sister.

"I think David is right. Momma needs this more than she can see."

"So how we going to handle this?"

"Don't you worry much. You leave the worrying to us smart folks.

"Man, please. You went to college in Alabama, okay? They still got recipes on how to hang Negroes in the school books there. You was a token. When you played football there they called you boy so much you thought it was alright."

"And now I am a city councilman. And you still a sales clerk."

"Assistant manager, with keys and benefits."

"An assistant manager. And that's cool to you."

"Cool as a fan with me. And that's my point. Let me live my life.'

"Not off of momma, not anymore."

"Yo, kill that. I ain't living off her and you need to stop saying that.

"Girls, I have someplace to be."

"Or what?" Adam ignored her.

"Or you going to get knocked the fuck out."

"STOP IT NOW! If we doing the party let's talk about that. You two can fight any damn time."

"Okay, just let me handle the details. We all chip in and Mardessa and I will get the goods and we party."

"If it ain't fixed don't broke it."

"Funny. You a clown."

"Right back at you, slick."

"How much are you chipping in again?"

The three are quiet.

"I thought so. So just shut up and let me handle this. This is going to be classy. Big and better. Dad's going to be looking down and say, shit, why didn't I do it like that."

David mockingly looked up wide eyed.

"That's not funny," Patricia groaned.

"Well," David clapped his hand, "love to be educated all morning, but unlike you two shiesters, I have a real job. Gotta go."

Patricia said, "I guess I need to call folks."

"I got that," Adam said. "I'll send out the invites and all. Don't worry."

David said 'bye to his sister and, "Later, Mr. Congressman."

Adam grabbed him by his shoulders, "I swear to you. I swear. This party is everything to me. Important like you wouldn't comprehend. If you fuck this up for me I will have to kill you."

"Negro, please."

14

A week passed in a blur for the Taylor clan.

Everyone in the family was busy getting ready; including Verdie. For her it was nothing physical; she spent the time getting her mind right.

When dawn arrived on the day before the party, Patricia found herself lying awake reflecting on her future. She too had to get her mind right.

She thought about when she met Marc, at a club of all places. She was in there on chill mode, with her girlfriends, kee-keeing and not really paying much attention to the men there that night. Most were gay, and dressed better than her and her friends, first off. And secondly she was less than a month removed from a knucklehead who posed as boyfriend material for three months.

She reveled in how Marc was into her that night. Then she discovered she had on a top that night that didn't close right. But, in her memory, his eyes were on hers the whole time.

She remembers her dad saying the most important key to communication with a man, a friend, or even God, was openness. You be open. I encourage you to be open, to love enough to be vulnerable. Be honest. See things like they are.

He said, "I encourage you to be open, to love enough to be vulnerable. Be honest. What the hell? Have fun in life but always try to see things like they are."

In the shower that morning she came up with the idea to take her mother shopping. She called her mother when she got out, and had to redial her because the first time Verdie didn't answer.

"You want to go shopping with me?"

Verdie sighed.

"Well, if you want, give me your list and I can do your shopping for you?" she asked blankly.

"No, you know what? Enough of the hibernation. I need to go."

Verdie finally thought she'd been holed-up inside her home for too long. She had to get out, be with people, and laugh with someone, if she ever hoped to go on living.

Patricia felt a sprinkle of good feelings. "I'll be there in an hour, we'll do lunch, all that."

Verdie took a quick shower, opting to layout her clothes after she dried her body.

When she opened her closet, Verdie decided immediately that she needed to choose something that would lift her spirits; she decided to wear her lucky color. She pulled on a pair of lavender slacks and a soft purple lamb's wool tank and sweater set to match.

When Patricia got there Verdie liked her daughter's outfit that morning. Patricia looked sleek and hippy in red and cream. Her baby was a clothes whore and she always looked attractive. If someone she knew caught her in old jeans, without makeup or her hair not done just right, she would respond like a vampire cornered by sunlight.

They invited Pauline, but she wasn't interested.

"I am not ready to go shopping. I go late, like the day of the party, every year. Better deals then," Grandmomma said.

"But the crowds, Momma. Why don't you come on and go with us."

"Uh uh. I do like I do."

"Grandmomma, we are going to do more than shop."

"The gossiping? We can do that later."

"Alrighty then. You do you."

"Thank you and good bye."

Just a few steps out of the house felt refreshing. Verdie took a deep breath and like the thought that she was living, and going on with life.

"I got a surprise," Patricia said as she moved her car out into traffic.

Verdie just smiled.

Patricia took her mother to get pampered. There had been a black spa that opened a few blocks from the house and Patricia called them that morning and got them an appointment for the works, her hair shampooed and set, a massage, and both a pedicure and manicure. This was all to go down after they finished shopping. And the works there included a full, three course lunch.

All the stores in the mall were decked out for Christmas with green and red and signs declaring big sales. Verdie liked the sights, the crowd was a good distraction, and she was finally feeling the spirit of the season. And then she saw the men's department in Macy's from outside in the mall. She even looked for the tie rack. It hurt, but not as deeply as she expected.

At the spa, during the lunch, their hair and bodies wrapped in thick terry cloth, Verdie thought about the fact that Patricia had been with one guy for awhile.

"How's Mr. Marcus?"

"Momma! Don't call him that. You listening to David."

Verdie laughed.

"And what you know about Mr. Marcus?"

"I have me a DVD player, chile."

"No! You a mess, and that is where David got it."

"Right. So how is Marcus?"

"I am thinking about letting him go. He is getting too serious too soon."

"No. I like this one."

"I know you want grandchildren and all that..."

Verdie sensed the pain. She wanted to yes, sure she does, especially from her baby girl.

"Marc is nice, I mean. He tells me how beautiful I am, how good I look, all the time. However, his compliments only make me angry. I think he is being insincere, trying to get some."

"One damn day he said, "He said he was afraid he was falling in love with me."

"Wow," Verdie chuckled. "I bet you smack the mess out of him for that!"

"Momma! I was like, what the eff? I didn't really know what he meant."

"Don't take it so seriously, just enjoy it. You like him don't you?"

"I do like him. But I don't know. It hasn't been a year and he loves me. What if he proposes?"

"Then, girlie, it's on and popping!"

"You gotta really kick David out of the house. Please."

Verdie fell back in her chair and laughed.

The sprinkles of joy in watching her caused Patricia to tear up. She swallowed some water as if it was lumpy."

"You okay, Tricia?"

"I love you, momma. And I miss daddy so."

"I miss him too. But I think he just wants us happy."

"I hope he is.'

"He is. He has made more friends than the group of angels that guide you through the gates of Heaven."

"Oh momma," Patricia got up and hugged her seated mother.

Verdie vowed not to shed any tears while out with Patricia and she was sticking to it. She stood up and held and patted her daughter and held her for as long as she needed to cry it out

The shopping trip, the day at the spa and the talk with her daughter was a complete success. Verdie wasn't depressed for long periods of time ever again.

15

Adam didn't want his wife to make everything; well, at least not all the finger food. She had already bought veggie and cheese trays from *Sam's Club*. Now they needed the Buffalo-style chicken wings.

They walked into a corner Chinese restaurant in an unsightly, decrepit strip mall in the hood. A place the couple surely looked out of place entering but a area his dad shopped often. Mao's was where his dad bought the wings for the party the past 11 years, since the place opened.

Mao had been smiling behind the counter, at the completion of sale, until he saw Adam come through the door He folded his arms and stood upright.

"Hi. I need to make that big order for the party. The usual, you know. I'll pick it up later."

"You father was such a good man." Mao said. "But you were always disrespectful."

"What? Please, with that."

"No MSG. Ha! Sign right there!" Mao pointed to the letters MSG in a red circle with a line through it. "*No bean sprout. Don't fry wings too hard. No Pork grease.* How about, *no food tonight*? How about, *no party food*?"

"What? Whatever," Adam went into his wallet and removed a hundred dollar bill. He waved it in the air. "Scurry back there and start making them chicken wings. You people addicted to the American dollar."

"Forget it, big shot. No party wings for you."

Mardessa shot out an angry sigh. "Let's go. He doesn't want your business so there is no sense arguing about it. I told you, we should spend our dollars with each other."

"That's right," Adam barked. "You stand there looking down on people that pay you. What am I begging this foreigner to take my money? You know what? We passed three black owned wings places to get to this cat cemetery. We going to shut you down!"

"We?" Mao glanced at Mardessa and then back to Adam. "You are not French and you have no friends. Take your speech out the door, big shot."

Adam waved and cursed going out.

Adam drove them to the Bert's Wing Hut, a trailer in the supermarket's lot, up the street from the Chinese restaurant. He and Mardessa get out of his luxury car.

Adam exhaled, "Why we go to a Chinese restaurant for hot wings in the first place?"

"Right."

"That don't make sense."

They get to the window.

Adam ordered, "I need to order 500 wings. Mix them, about twenty of each kind."

The woman at the counter frowned. "Five hundred wings? What, y'all having a party?"

"Exactly. Now I just need..."

"That's a lot of work. I don't know. What Time you need them?"

"Right. Seven or eight would be good."

She shook her head. "I am trying to close early tonight. I can't do it."

"What? You don't feel like working? How you plan to stay in business?"

"Good bye, sir. Come back tomorrow."

"That is a damn shame," Mardessa said.

"This is getting ridiculous."

They slammed themselves into Adam's SUV. Reluctantly, he drove two blocks to the Wing Castle, another trailer in the lot of a gas station.

Now Mardessa was frowning. "I don't know about this place."

"We just getting some wings. How could they mess that up?"

"Easily. I mean, dang, it's a dump. Do they even have a health department report? What could their score be. Minus seven."

Adam groaned a long sigh.

"Maybe we could try Publix or Kroger."

"Grocery store wings? Oh no." Shaking his head, he saw that people are walking away in disgust. He decided to go see what was up and give them some business.

Mardessa didn't go with him.

"We don't have anymore wings. We got fish, hamburgers."

"This place is called Wing Castle. How you run out of wings?'

"The owner didn't bring enough to day."

"What? Insane."

The woman suddenly smiled brightly, "Hey, aren't you the Taylor boy that just became a Congressman?"

"Councilman."

"Whatever. I've been to your daddy's Christmas party. Nice. Best one I ever been too."

"Yeah."

"Sorry he passed. Good man."

"Yeah. Thanks. So no wings?"

"No wings."

Adam walked away. Mardessa followed.

The woman at the counter said good bye but Adam didn't respond.

In the truck he said, "We have to go to Mao's."

"Thought you didn't want to go there."

He just sighed.

"This is madness."

"I'll make the wings."

"You?"

"Yes. I can cook them while I do everything else. Just run me by the grocery store."

It made sense to Adam. This should have been the plan from jump, he was thinking.

<u>*16*</u>

Mother and daughter come home to find David and his boy LaQuan tearing up the vestibule with the Christmas tree the grandmother had hand-picked.

The young men were struggling and cursing. They moved the tree aside so Patricia and Verdie can get into the house.

"They are having fun, aren't they," Verdie said to her mother.

"The fools helping Mary with the tree for baby Jesus didn't curse this much, and it was cold and snowing outside back at the first tree rising."

Verdie turned to the boys. "You guys need help?"

"Nah, not at all. We messing it up just fine by ourselves."

"Good," Patricia said, stepping out of the way.

"My Lord? Next time get the big one."

"Oh, mother," David said from outside. "The humor is so helpful."

"Be careful, now."

Patricia said, "May I suggest cutting the tree in half?"

"Funny. Tricia Chappelle over there. No, please don't help us."

"Okay, I won't."

LaQuan whined, "Dude, it's too big."

"That's just what your girl told me. I'ma tell you the same thing I told her. It'll fit."

"Whatever."

"It ain't too big. You have to take your end up the steps and I'll turn the bottom into the living room."

"I can't get a grip. You gonna have to push."

David pushed it hard. The tree overwhelmed LaQuan and ran him over.

David laughed. "Sorry, pimpin'. My bad."

LaQuan's curses and bitching was muffled by the tree. Adam arrived behind LaQuan. He stepped in over them and the tree.

"Clef and Def. You two are doing an excellent job."

"Thanks, congressman." David said while showing his middle finger.

"Why didn't you get the big one?"

"Ho larious," David said from under the tree's top. "You stealing your mother's jokes."

Adam found his mother on the sofa unboxing the ornaments.

He plants a soft kiss on Verdie's forehead. "How can you get anything done with all the struggling and foul language, dear mother?"

"Faggot," one of the boys yelled from the doorway.

"I heard that," Verdie said. "That wasn't nice."

"It wasn't me momma. I generally like those people."

"David?"

They finally got it in while Adam walked by to the kitchen.

"Wait, hold up," David told LaQuan. "All your hard breathing is fogging the foyer. "Where's it going, ma?"

"Don't act brand new. You know where it's going. Where it goes every year."

Ten minutes later they had the tree in its spot and in the stand.

They all stood in front of the tree.

"What do you think, David. It look straight to you?"

"It's where you're standing."

"It look straight to me."

"I am legally blind and I can see it's as crooked as a dog's hind legs."

"Move it a little to the left."

"Right there! Stop! There it goes."

Grandmomma nodded. "The fools got it."

"I don't know. I guess it's fine. I just don't want to have another accident like 2001."

"What happened in 2001?"

"You don't remember? The tree fell over on Mr. Mason and his hair piece got stick in the branches.

LaQuan laughed. "Oh yes. He was salty for awhile. He don't come no more, right."

"Nope."

Verdie, Patricia and the boys decorated the tree while Grandmomma drank spiked Egg Nog. They had a really good time, drinking wine and telling stories about past parties.

"Light her up!" Verdie said and David plugged in the lights and the tree illuminated in flying colors. Verdie stepped back and admired the sight.

"How it look?" David said.

"It's beautiful."

"That's what your girl said!" LaQuan giggled.

No one else laughed.

"Damn," Patricia said, "you stupid and inappropriate."

"That's what his girl said," David added.

LaQuan just kept on laughing.

17

Thursday morning, the day of the Christmas Party, Verdie climbed out of bed with a vicious head cold. Her eyes were red, her nose just as red.

Verdie slept deeply for two hours, and then she drifted up through a layer of sleep and began to dream. She was at her parents' house and the air was filled with delicious smells and the atmosphere was warm and inviting. Her mother and aunts were cooking. Everyone in the dream was dead, and she was there not as a 12 year old as she should have been with all them alive, but she was herself now.

And it wasn't Christmas, it was Easter. But Teddy, looking young and handsome, like the day they met, wanted to have a tree. "Rabbits like trees too," he argued. "And ain't this just another Jesus holiday like in December?"

A usual morning look out the window and she discovered it was snowing. Coming down like diamond dust, in light, puffy feather-like flakes. A white Christmas would be a nice thing up North but snow was not a good thing in Atlanta.

This was perfect, she thought with a smile before a cough killed the grin. Her excuse was made for her. She'd tell her children that she was too ill to host the party. Then she considered thought this is a much needed holiday. Her husband's favorite holiday. Verdie used to love doing all the things that make Christmas special. And this swiftly she hated the holiday.

She thought about Christmas being on a Saturday and that would have delighted Teddy. He would have tried to have the party go the whole weekend.

As she gathered all her strength into her arms,

In her racy robe and fleece-lined slippers she shuffled downstairs to make herself some hot tea. She ached from head to toe but she was going to do this. She was going to help make this holiday happen. This was what her husband would have wanted-for the party to go on.

By the time she finished her high fiber breakfast, the temperature rose and all the nice white snow had turned water.

She went back into her room and her eyes caught on the stack of presents on her floor. She carried them out to the living room and diligently began wrapping.

Verdie's stack of presents filled out the tree by the time her son and mother awoke. They both appeared in the living room at the same time.

"Breakfast?"

"I just want one egg, nothing special," Grandmomma said.

"Me and Quan are going to grab something out," David said. "I gotta go scoop up Quan."

"Simple fool," Grandmomma said.

"He needs to finish the lights before dark."

"Among other slave work we got for the imbecile."

"Lincoln freed the slaves, Grandmomma."

"And I brought just him back."

Verdie cut in, "You are going to need to make sure to salt down the front and back porch. I don't need *your* relatives slipping and falling and then suing."

"Gotcha, momma." David moved in and kissed her and then his Grandmomma. "See y'all in a minute."

When David got back, LaQuan went right into decorating the house while David began stacking the living room's bar from his dad's booze cabinet in the basement. He was stringing up the lights around the shrubbery bushes. He turned back at his creation to realize the lights are tangled as bad weave.

David lugged cases of liquor up the steps, making four trips. He then went into the kitchen and got the ingredients and the bowl to make the mixed fruit punch. He was supposed to make two, one with and one without alcohol. But as per tradition, his dad's doing, he made both with booze. He dad didn't trust grown ups that didn't drink alcohol. After David set up the various liquor bottles on the bar his grandmother appeared while he was pouring vodka in the punch bowl labeled 'non-alcohol'...he then took a swig from the bottle.

His grandmother took up a cup.

"None until the party starts, Grandmomma."

She poked her middle finger up at him.

David went outside to find LaQuan now had lights tangled around his neck and torso, fighting with the string of lights as they flash off and on

"Oh, you got that alright," David said before going back into the house.

David soon found out he had to take his grandmother shopping. He was pissed, it being the two days before Christmas, but he had to do it. He and Grandmomma come outside to find LaQuan drinking a beer and admiring his work.

"My sweet Lord in Christ," Grandmomma said clutching her pearls. "What the...?"

The lights were mixed around and crooked in no detectable design.

"Grandmomma, this is what happens when we hire the mentally challenged from AA."

"It's straight," LaQuan said.

"Straight like a punch to your head."

Patricia knew what she wanted to wear. She had laid out her clothes moments after getting out of the bed. She just couldn't get herself to get dressed.

The dress she had selected was one her mother never liked but it highlighted all her assets. First of all it was red; Verdie was against red dresses for any occasion. It had a deep neckline and was above the knee. It hugged her hips and flared to the legs.

She had the strappy heels on the floor under the dress.

She lost an hour watching the news, then another half hour after turning the channel to a comedy.

Then Marc called. And she liked that he did. There was no one else she'd rather talk to right then.

"I am just sitting here, in my bra and panties. I can't make a move."

"Hey now," although he could hear the hurting in her voice, he joked. "I should come right over."

She laughed. She knew he was busy today, and knew he would come if he could, and she felt instantly comforted.

"Baby, just throw on some jeans and sneakers and go on over there. Take the dress with you. Maybe that is it, you just feel anxious about it all right now. You'll be fine once you get there."

"Yeah, maybe so."

She thanked him some and they chatted for a second before she did just that and rode over to her moms.

At Adam's crib, he was trying on different ties, all his dad's, posing himself suavely in the mirror. With each one he doesn't like with his cream suit with subtle green pinstripes, he frustratingly yanked it off.

"I'll wear dad's Christmas tie," he says to himself. His dad never wore it, although Reynolds made it especially for the Christmas party. No, Teddy only dressed up during the weekdays, while he was working. Adam put his suit jacket on and smiled at himself in the mirror.

"Dude, you ready. This is it. See the ball, hit the ball."

"I have everything packed and ready to roll. The appetizers are done, the rest is prepped and ready to cook."

"Then you know what, fine wife of mine, we ready for this."

<u>*18*</u>

Adam and Mardessa came into the house carrying many bags of groceries.

Verdie was at the sink washing vegetables.

Patricia was putting the beers into three coolers of ice.

They shared hellos.

"Where's lazy boy?" Adam asked. "He's hiding now that it's time to work?"

Verdie shook her head, "That's not nice. He took your grandmother to Rich's to get a wig. Then by her place to get the food she made for the party."

"Better him than me."

Verdie grinned.

Adam came behind his mother and kissed her on the cheek. "Mother, I am going to be mayor."

"I have no doubt."

"And this Christmas party, Dad's party, should seal it. I have invited some big wigs. We doing it."

Mardessa came in her cream dress that Verdie just loved, but her bitterness to the young woman kept her from saying it. Her eyes, though, betrayed her.

"You like?" Mardessa twirled. I got it on sale."

"It is nice."

"$1700. Dior."

"Hmm."

"And I bought this apron from Louis Vutton."

"Alrighty then."

"I am ready for this. It's going to be great."

"Yes ma'am, it should be."

"I already set out the appetizers. We are just about ready to get this going."

Mardessa's smile was the biggest and brightest Verdie has seen on the young lady since the day Mardessa married her son.

Mardessa sorted through all of the utensils in the draws, and then cupboards for ingredients. She was prepping her kitchen in impressive fashion, even Verdie had to admit.

Aunt BeBe had come early to offer help. She had been far from her sister since Thanksgiving. She just could not come up with the right words to console her sister. Teddy's death hit Bebe hard as well; she loved the way he loved her sister, and could never find that love for herself.

Verdie was observing how Mardessa prepared the food for the evening. She tried not to be in the way or be critical, but she was wide-eyed and analytical. She quietly watched Mardessa use a full bottle of jelly and no hot sauce on the drumettes; but when she saw her put Ranch dressing in the deviled eggs she had to ask.

"What?" Mardessa asked first; she could almost hear the thoughts in her mother-in-law's head.

"That's interesting. Ranch?"

"It's my secret ingredient. Now you know. I may have to kill you," she giggled.

"Oh, I won't tell."

Verdie and Bebe moved through the kitchen and to the living room.

Bebe just had to ask, "Ah, and why is there another woman in your kitchen?"

"Ah uh, don't you dip into this, okay? I am getting a rest this year."

"Really now?"

"Silent night from you."

19

David, LaQuan and Grandmomma reached David's truck in the crowded mall's parking lot. David set the bags into the back while they got in.

As soon as they got into the exiting lane they were stalled in thick traffic. David sighed, elbow on his window, his head on his hand. "Sheesh. Ten minutes to shop and two hours to commute. I love the holidays."

LaQuan chuckled. "It's Christmas, playboy. Shoulda known better."

"Thanks. You smarter."

They moved slowly to the main street and then once again are jammed up.

His grandmother broke the silence. "Davey, I know what I want for Christmas, baby."

"What's that, Granny?"

His grandmother got upset suddenly. "Now, now, I told you not to call me that. I am nobody's granny. Makes me sound like an old woman."

LaQuan giggled. He turned around and said, "And what are you?"

"Don't mess with her, please?" David pleaded.

"I don't need any backup for Shim," Grandmomma said, "I am going to have to knock him in the head."

"Shim?"

"Yes, girlie boy."

David raised his voice, "What do you want from Christmas?'

" I want that Hooker DBD."

"DBD?"

"The movie thingy."

DVD?"

"Yes, don't get smart."

"What, girls gone wild?" LaQuan said excitedly. "Nah, for real?"

"What the hell I want that crap for? Preschool dumb niggers. I am talking about the TV show with Captain Kirk."

David thought it through. "Oh, you mean TJ Hooker?"

"You like correcting me. Keep it up. The DBD is out and I want it. Get it."

"Ah, yeah. You didn't think to mention that while we were in the crowded ass mall?"

She whacked him upside his head with an open hand.

"I'm driving here, Grandmomma!"

"We not moving. You can get hit at anytime being fresh with me. Note that for next time."

LaQuan was laughing. He turned to the back and said, "But why you say DBD? It's D V D."

She calmed herself, just blinking at LaQuan's big-tooth grin.

"Ha ha! DBD."

"Who claims this fool? Because when I crack his skull wide open and bloody, I need to know who to send a reef too."

"Calm down granny, with the talk of violence."

She popped LaQuan harder than she had hit her flesh and blood.

"You sure know how to handle women, pimpin'."

"She know I don't fight 'em, just love 'em. But, playboy, look at buddy's car." LaQuan points to a souped-up Chevy Impala.

"Sweet," David said. "Candy apple red."

"Clean."

Grandmomma sucked her false teeth. "Are you two homosexuals?"

"What?" David's head spun and his face was in a grimace.

LaQuan turned and looked at her and then back to his boy, "Your grandmother is straight tripping, homie."

"What the heck you ask us something like that for?" David laughed. "You think we can't fight?"

"Neither one of you like women."

David just laughed,

LaQuan got upset. "Now I know you wrong for that, Grammie."

"Don't call me no Grammie, sissy."

David was laughing big time now.

"Sissy?" LaQuan turned back to her. "No, hold up. I love me a woman, *Grand Ma*. What just 'cause I don't be, what, having them around you? You don't see me. You can't see me. You don't even go out at night."

David shook his head, "Calm down."

"No, see, he's yelling. You getting mad, faggot boy."

"Hold up, she is going to chill with that."

"Sissy."

"Grandmomma, okay? Please?"

"Yo!"

"Sissy."

David leaned forward on his steering wheel in the stand-still traffic while the argument grew.

"...and David baking cookies like a good little daughter."

David shook his head. "I thought this was between you two?"

"Yo, for real, playboy," LaQuan said. "Grammie right here, she can walk home while us sissies ride out."

Grandmomma turned her head to look out her window.

"I thought so," LaQuan declared victory.

Grandmomma kicked his seat, "Sissy."

20

At the house, things are just about set for the first Taylor's Christmas party without Teddy.

The scenes from room to room were...Mardessa struggling with four things cooking at once, utterly overwhelmed but she was trying to seem calm...Verdie wrapped the last present and placed it at the top of the stack of colorful gifts...David set out the nuts, pretzels and chips about the bar...LaQuan had clean up duty, and he grimaced as he reached the kitchen with a large bag of trash.

"What the hell is that smell?"

Mardessa shot him a look filled with daggers.

Patricia sat down, thinking she should be doing something. But there was nothing for her to do. Mardessa had control of the kitchen and the men were doing everything else. She knew to be early, and to tell Marc to come much later. She didn't want to deal with his loving eyes while she was busy, while the party was in full swing, but now all she could think about was how he had soothed her soul so easily.

The sound of her grandmother Grandmomma does spit take on Mac and cheese. "No milk, no flavor. Loooord. Who made these," she asked.

"You granddaughter in-law."

"Remind me not to eat these."

"Grandmomma!"

"At least she is overly beautiful, 'cause she can't cook worth no damn."

Adam snapped her into another reality, "Where's your brother?"

"He went to his room, I think."

Adam found David looking through the closet of his bedroom.

"I know you got some weed."

"Negro, do not do that. I could have killed you. Don't sneak up on me."

"Yo, roll that shit up."

"You being nosy again. What you doing down here?"

"I bought me some gators, special order jammies."

He pulled down the box off the shelf to show David.

"Brown?"

"Sand and tea."

"Brown and beige?"

"You a lame."

"Why you not rocking them? Oh, thems don't look like gators."

"Don't be a racist. They came UPS. I had them come here.

David packed the weed in his jacket. "You and your shit and piss colored boots be happy. I am going upstairs."

They ran into their Momma.

"What you boys doing?"

"Momma, whoa? Is that a new dress. Is that my momma looking sexy as hell?"

"Boy stop. I already got your gift."

David smooched her forehead.

Verdie said, "And I thought I told you to salt the back porch?"

"Momma, I so forgot. My bad."

"Your bad? Take care of that now."

"Right away, sexy momma, right away."

"That boy so full of shit his eyes are brown," Adam said as David moved away.

"And I love you too, Congressman!"

21

The doorbell rang and everybody knew it was on and popping.

Adam, Patricia, Mardessa and Verdie came to alert.

"I'll get it!" Adam yelled. He did a dash to the front door, knocking David out of the way. "this is me right here."

"Damn you a shine."

Patricia laughed. "What, he thinks we are going to say the wrong thing at the door?

Adam opened the door to reveal a well dressed Caucasian couple Stanley and Susan Hall.

"Hey, good to see you, Stan, Susan. Come in, come in."

Hi there. Merry Christmas."

"Thank you, Go ahead an have a seat."

Adam took their coats and before he could put them down the doorbell rang again, this time he could see more people walking up, and cars parking. He couldn't help but be excited.

After a few trips to his mother's room with coats, he found the spacious living room is now filled with bodies and chatter. Most of the seats are taken.

"How is everybody? The food should be done pretty soon."

People nod and chide. They seem content.

Patricia wondered, "Why are they here so early?"

"I told them six, and told the Negroes eight. Which means the white people could enjoy themselves in peace until 10 when the coloreds come."

"Adam, please," Verdie was shaking her head. "talking like that."

Mardessa laughed.

Patricia said, "And that was why you wanted to handle the invites? That's foul."

"Don't be mad because I am smarter."

David came in, "Mr. Whiteman Lover, er, I'ma put the music on. You see my Kurtis Blow CD?"

"No, no, no. No rap, no rap, no rap," Adam said. "I brought music. I got this."

"Whatever."

They walk out and Adam brought out his CD case. He puts in a mixed jazz Christmas CD. David looked through them, "What the heck is all this? You robbed Jimmy Carter's library?"

"No. I got this. Don't you fret none."

"No. You do not.

David craned his neck to see what music Adam was choosing to play. "Bing Crosby Christmas? Leann Rimes? Aw, hell naw. Playboy, no."

"Black person yes. No rap, no rap, no rap."

"Where is the Kurtis Blow CD?"

"What I say? No rap."

"That ain't rap, that is a tradition."

"No rap."

"You playing yourself. You freaking out. A Black man in a suit is still what I am."

"Don't hate. Go help with the food."

"Dude, you going to have to play some good music sooner or later." David moved into the kitchen. He came back with some food trays.

"Oh, good, slave boy. You got the Mac and cheese and the anti-pasta? Nice."

"That ain't funny with all your white people around."

"You people are sensitive," Adam laughed.

"Yeah. I thought you were one of us. But this crap your wifey made, I don't think that is Mac and cheese."

"It is, put it there."

"You making plates for your guest?"

"That's how I do it."

"You feeding your guest? I thought it was buffet style, get your own."

LaQuan cut in, "Unless you white."

David and LaQuan laughed.

"Morons.

David shrugged, "This is what you gotta do to be mayor, I guess."

"The party is on and snapping," Adam said rubbing his hands together.

22

Suddenly, there was a commotion in the living room that startled the Taylor's in the kitchen. Conversations had turned loud, and there were gasping sounds.

David was wondering about the cursing and gagging over the jazzy Christmas music, He walked in from his bedroom and saw people were bolting for the front door, searching for their coats and yelling for directions to the nearest bathroom. He noticed people were getting sick.

LaQuan said to him, "The first guy in the bathroom locked the door."

"What the?"

"Dave, man," LaQuan was pointing with his thumb, "y'all killing your guest. There's a line to the bathroom, people throwing up like they at a Mase concert."

David walked to the hall as if in a trance. People are banging on the door. "Damn. Listen, we have two bathrooms upstairs, another in the room on the left and another in the basement."

People separated in a hurry.

LaQuan walked up. "Y'all done brought Sal Minella to the party, player."

David came into the kitchen in a hurry.

"What's going on out there?" Verdie smiled, "They dancing? It's kinda quiet."

Before he could say, Adam rushed in faster and blurted, "I think we have a food situation here," he said.

"Oh God," Verdie exhaled. "People are getting sick from the food?"

"Seems that way to me," David said. "Has to be the food. They ain't drank nothing that fast."

Verdie and Patricia ventured into the living room. Besides Marc sitting there looking amused, it was empty. Most people were at the bathrooms or trying to leave. She moved to the food table and looked closely. Verdie jumped, "Whoa. What the? This ain't sweet potatoes. It's Mac and cheese.

"Is that's what that's supposed to be?" Patricia covered her laugh. "Wow."

"Oh my. She has put marshmallow and raisins in the macaroni and cheese?"

She checked over the other dishes. "And the anti-pasta salad is drenched in vinegar," she whispered.

"Yuck. And the wings ain't done," Patricia added. Her fork revealed blood red chicken meat to the bone. "My God."

In the kitchen, they confronted Mardessa with their findings and she suddenly cried out and became completely hysterical.

Verdie and Patricia tried to console her. David and Adam looked on with bowed heads. Mardessa had a fistful of wet tissue.

David suggested, "Maybe we should call 911."

Adam kicked him.

"This is so terrible..." Mardessa was saying, "I could have killed somebody."

"No, no. No one's dying."

"Not yet," David said. He was sick in another way.

Mardessa tried to explain, "Maybe the chicken wasn't done...I was doing too many things at once."

"Maybe?" Patricia shook her head.

"So, yes, blame me."

Grandmomma slowly shook her head and gave off some ums. Quietly, she disappeared down into the basement.

Adam was near tears, his hands covering his face. He bent his body as if suffering in pain. "My career is dead."

David scoffed, "Over bad food at a party?"

"Bad food?" Mardessa said.

David gulped. "I didn't mean any offense."

"It was taken. You are offensive. Pig."

"Hey, hold up. Don't talk to my brother like that. He didn't mean..."

"You don't speak to me like that! Don't scold me like I am some child."

"Hold up," David said. "I am sorry it came out like that, for real. I didn't mean anything.

"Why don't you just shut up? You come in here criticizing and you haven't contributed squat.

"Shutting up."

Mardessa storms out.

Adam lets her leave. He is more worried about his future than his wife and brother's argument.

David offers his hand. "I didn't mean any disrespect, dude."

"I know that," Adam takes it and stands. They hug.

The sound of people gagging and vomiting entered the kitchen.

"My Lord," Verdie sighed. "Let me go check on the guests."

"Shit," David grunted as it all hit him again.

"It's going to be alright. Not everybody is here yet, we can get rid of the sick folks, get some new food and party on.

"I'm with that."

Adam fell into a chair at t he kitchen table. "Shit. Man, I am done."

"Yeah, you are done, for tonight. Relax. Why don't you go after your wife, do something you can handle."

"She ain't going no where. The car is blocked in."

He was right. After Mardessa rustled her coat free from under the stack of coats on Verdie's bed, she bolted through the house then she was out the door.

23

Verdie was at her front door helping the white guests to leave; gathering their coats and handing out wet wipes to those that had messed on themselves. She apologized, like a good host of a bad party.

People were whispering angrily as the snatch their coast and bullied by her.

Adam, standing next to his mom at the door, was saying, "I'm deadly sorry," while shaking hands.

LaQuan was shaking his head. He said to Adam, "That's how you treat your white folks?"

"You stupid little something. Just shut your mouth."

LaQuan laughed.

Adam caught the eye of Congressman Sweeney. The Congressman had held back to make sure he was the last of the VIP guest to speak bitter goodbyes at the door.

"Now those people are coming," he sighed.

Adam thought he hadn't heard right.

"You okay?" Sweeney said. He had his coat on.

"Yes. You, and the wife?"

"We are fine, didn't have that much. We had eaten out before coming."

"I'm glad you didn't get sick."

"Oh, don't worry about this. It happens. Some of us can't handle that heavy seasoning you people use."

Adam almost laughed; he couldn't though. His mind was too tight.

"You are going to be fine, people now have a story to tell, and it will be a comedy by next year this time."

"Good, I'll be laughed at."

They watched David hustling to get the clean up going.

"Too bad that bum is your brother. Besides that you'll have a great campaign." He said while slipping a thick envelope into Adam's . "In there is not only my endorsement but a substantial joint effort to get you in that seat at city Hall."

"You know what?" Adam grabbed hold of his own crotch, "if you want a puppet pull this string."

Sweeney looked in Adam's eyes. "This is your reply?"

Adam dropped the envelope and shook his head. "Go on home out of my face."

"I am sorry you feel this way."

"Yeah you are. Go get with your wife and step on."

Adam stepped away. He saw Sweeney bend for the money.

Verdie watched the argument with mixed feelings. Happy her son finally saw the light, and thrilled, a bit, that he had told off a man her late husband never had.

She came from behind her son. She rubbed her hands high up on his tall shoulders. "You was all about having a good time. Trying to make it something it wasn't. Just be yourself. You don't have to be him, and you don't have to impress anyone looking at you to be him."

David and Patricia worked swiftly, cleaning up the messes caused by the bad food. They were wiping, moping and cleansing all they could; it was the bathroom and the floor outside of it that was hit the worst. They did, and did it quickly to keep from their mother feeling like she had to.

All David wanted to do while his sister walked around spraying the house with air freshener, was to sit down. But then he found LaQuan's dumb behind eating the bad food.

"Oh, my God. How you eating that?"

"What?"

LaQuan looked up, his lips and fingers were greasy.

David felt his stomach churn and his mouth went dry. "Dude, what, you took that out the garbage?"

"You bugging." LaQuan used his tongue to clean his face, and then licked his fingers.

"Dude, you making me sick.'

"Huh? Go on away from here, now."

"You crazy, don't eat that. That's the bad..."

"Fool, you staggerin'. This some good eating. Them woods can't handle our food. You know that. They systems ain't ready for the seasoning."

"Christ the king. That leg right there is bleeding."

"That's the sauce. Stop the dramatics."

The bleeding chicken, the greasy lips, David was about ready to hurl.

"I'ma be outside, kid. My God."

LaQuan popped up two fingers as to say *Peace.*

24

Grandmomma caught David standing watching folks leaving.

"Hey hump. Get the sissy and you two come down to the basement and give me a hand."

"Hump? Dang, I thought I was your favorite?"

"Quit the whining."

The three of them went down and found that Grandmomma had stashed food in the basement's refrigerator. She had made Swedish meatballs, a chicken salad and deviled eggs.

They brought it all up to the kitchen.

"Momma!" Verdie grinned brightly. "You done saved the day."

"How does David say it, that's how I do it? Well, that is how I do it. Making y'all look good. A full time job."

They all laugh, except Adam. He moved out of the kitchen.

"Heat up them meatballs," Grandmomma said. "The rest is ready to go. Now we can eat and live, like the honorable Elijah Muhammad said."

"Huh?" LaQuan said.

"Shut up. Don't correct me and get hurt about it."

This ain't gonna be enough food, David was thinking.

David snatched up the kitchen wall's phone. He dialed quickly.

"Hey, Mao. This is Taylor's son. We having that party and we really need to make a order to pick up.

"Teddy's son? Which one?"

"Come on, Mao. It's me, David."

"Oh, come. I am so sorry about your father. What a good man. Food will be ready in 15 minutes."

"I need at least a hundred. And some Lo Mien."

"Come."

"You da man, Mao."

"Yes, I know this. And Davey, do not bring your brother."

Reynolds approached the kitchen on soft steps. When Verdie turned to see him she felt a sharp slice at her heart. The only time she ever saw the man he was with Teddy.

"Season's Greetings, "Reynolds said quietly. He had a slim, thick wooden case across both hands. He held it out for Verdie. Verdie was stunned silent and lost her smile. She knew only a tie could be in such a case.

The kitchen fell silent and no one moved, all eyes were on the case.

She looked, opened it and inside was a shiny golden tie. It looked like it costs a million bucks, and when she touched it the fabric seemed to melt in her hands.

"Oh, Reynolds."

"For my favorite client. I will miss him. He will be missed."

"Oh. Beautiful."

"He was bugging me to do one like that the last two years. It's not my style, but it is his. So sorry it was, is, too late."

Verdie was shaking her head, "No. It's fine. It's okay.

"But you see I wasn't going to do it. What he didn't understand. Is that I only do this kind of work for presidents. My best work has hung in the closets of the white house. And I wanted this to be his when he got there."

"I...thank you."

"No, thank you."

They hugged.

Grandmomma was right behind them, vying for a peek at the tie. Verdie held it lower so she can see. She looked; then nonchalantly shrugged her shoulders. "Shit, it's too late now. He gone and buried." And she walked away.

Reynolds shook his head.

Adam opened the front door to leave out and find his wife. He ran into his brother's co-worker with a man in a wheelchair and a female in tow. The woman's sexy legs were revealed from her coat and when Adam looked up to her face her eyes said, 'I'm easy to know.'

He ignored the look and said hi to Ginata.

Ginata came close for a hello hug. "Merry Christmas," she said.

She introduced her friend, but Adam's mind was elsewhere. He did notice that the ladies would need help getting the guy and his chair up the four steps and into the house. He had Ginata take the handles and he lifted the chair by the wheels. The guy thanked him.

"Go on in and have a good time. We are still cooking in the kitchen."

They came in and Ginata spoke, "Hi everyone. Merry Christmas."

They were greeted back by the few people in the living room, except LaQuan who just stared open mouthed, plate in lap, mouth full and lips greasy.

"Hello LaQuan."

He just stood the mouth agape.

"What's the matter?"

"He greedy and eating again," Grandmomma said.

"Err ah, no nothing. Nothing of course. Um, have a seat. Let me go get Dave."

LaQuan dashed into the kitchen. He grabbed his boy, "Yo, you gotta come see Ginata's man."

"I'm a little busy right now. I ain't got time to see who you done fell in love with."

"No, for real, you gotta see buddy."

David became curious. "Is he a pretty boy or something?"

LaQuan shook his head.

"We know him?"

"Hell to the naw."

Verdie gave him an order before LaQuan got him moving, "When you go out there tell people we'll have some food out in a second."

LaQuan dragged him to the living room.

"Holy crip he's a crapple."

LaQuan busted out in laughter and fell back to the kitchen.

Ginata pushed her friend in his wheelchair to an open spot in the living room that had been occupied by the sick ones. She spoke to David, her voice softened into whisper suddenly.

"Hey," David replied. He was done looking at the dude in the wheelchair when he noticed the revealing dress Ginata was rocking as she slipped out of her long wool coat. The dress was a red halter with full circle skirt that stopped above her knee. And the strap black high heel sandals highlighted a pair of curvy legs he never knew existed.

"Damn," he said too loudly.

David shook off her body; he had Yvette coming and he had to address the growing crowd of party people.

"Ah, we had some bad food, it got ditched, we are moving on. More food, good food, to come. Quan, baby, saddle up. We rolling."

"Bad food?" Ginata asked.

"Yes. I will not be taking questions at this time. Have fun, drink some booze. And don't eat until I return. Thank you. You are all beautiful. As you were."

"What in the world?" someone exhaled.

LaQuan leaned in to Ginata and her friend, "Don't talk nobody or take no numbers while I'm gone. I'm deadly serious. I'm marrying you. You my type. You don't need to talk to nobody else. Period."

"Oh really now?"

"I can tell by your eyes that we are a match."

"Oh really?" Caren shook her head.

"Yes, ma'am. Me and you."

"Okay."

"What's your sign? You a Scorpio, right? Most fine females is that sign."

"What?" Ginata said.

"No. I am a Virgo," Caren said.

"Oh, you a Virgo You ain't do nothing yet?"

"Fast ball, inside corner, strike three! Now let's go."

Grandmomma was admiring the wheelchair.

She had to ask, "That's what I need. How is it on steps? The last one I had broke down."

The guy in the chair raised his eyebrows and shook his head.

25

Adam stepped outside. He was surprised that he was greeted with a cold gush of air. But the eyes of his wife were bitter and frigid.

Mardessa leaned on his luxury SUV, tapping a toe, her arms folded. She said, "Nice of you to rush out and see about me."

"Come on, come on back inside."

"These cars are blocking me in."

"Then stay awhile."

"It won't be long," she cut her eyes from him to the cars. "No, maybe these cars belong to the people I tried to kill and they are leaving.

"Stop it. It wasn't you. It was a mistake. Honest mistake."

"You know what? I tried. Your family is your family. I can't get into them."

"What? I mean..."

"No, you don't like them either so don't expect me to tolerate them?"

"Hold up. You see, I love them, they do some wrong, but I mean, they family."

"Get these cars out of the way. And are you coming with?"

"We are not leaving."

"Don't tell me what to do. There isn't anyone that wants me in there. So we are leaving. Or I am leaving. I don't care. Come or don't come. Stay with them, I don't care."

"Jesus, okay? Stop the drama for a second."

"How dare you?"

"Fuck," Adam sighed. "I am ruined and this is what I get?"

"Yeah, worry about your little predicament."

"You're saying I'm selfish?"

"No, I didn't say that. But your brother would."

Adam sighed deeply.

"Look. I want to talk about this later, I do, but right now I just need you to be with me. Me and my family. Fuck what happened earlier. Fuck the food, fuck it all, for real. I love you, you my wife, and them, they my family and this is the Christmas party. It is bigger than us, bigger than being mayor, bigger than any fight."

Mardessa softened at the thought of how much the party meant to the whole Taylor family and she considered his father.

She smiled and gently said, "So you still love me?"

"Damn right," he moved in and she let him take hold of her slender body. "That ain't the first time you done burnt dinner."

"Ah!" she jabbed him in his gut.

Adam kissed her and she opened up. She wrapped her arms around his neck and kissed him back.

Karl Rand arrived on the scene just as Adam was kissing Mardessa.

Karl married Teddy's baby sister Mary. He hated Teddy from day one, he didn't like how Teddy kept an eye on Mary. Teddy made sure she gave her love, and her body, wisely.

"Ain't y'all got a home to make out in?" Karl barked.

"Hey Uncle Karl, Aunt Mary. We married, we can make out anywhere."

"What is she looking at?" Karl said of Mardessa.

"Karl?" his wife bellowed.

He whispered, "Spoiled Adam probably bought her a mink and the BMW she sitting that flat ass on."

They were at the porch now. He stopped to say, "Y'all done spent all your daddy's money?"

Adam paid him no attention. He was into his wife, his hands going up and down her body.

Karl shook his head at the Mercedes in the driveway. "What the fuck?"

"Karl, leave it alone."

"That's the girl's," he tells his wife. "She had a damn Jap mobile before Teddy passed. Now she is in some new, different kinda foreign car. What the fuck?"

"Let them live. They were his children."

"Fuck that. Where's the rest of your money he left you. They spending it."

"Oh, I am sick of hearing that." She stopped following him. "Why we going up the back? Why can't we just go in the front and stop snooping around?"

"We here, what we going to all the way back around?"

He moved swiftly and slipped on a patch of ice he never saw. He fell right on his ass in a terrible bunch of noise.

26

The ride to Mao's was quiet. David was used to rolling with his boy in silence.

David checked on LaQuan. "Yo, you alive?"

"Dave, man, pull over."

"You gonna hurl? Hold on!"

"No, piss. Like a retarded race horse."

"For real, you can't hold it?"

"Ah, no, is my answer."

"Shit."

David eased over into a dark side street before the strip mall.

LaQuan jumped out and prepared to urinate. Just then a police patrol car approached on the main street.

"Dude?"

"Shit, I see." He stood still.

The car passed them.

"Fuck!"

"What?"

David looked out and saw LaQuan's pants were wet, thick and dark. David laughed. "No, dog, no. Oh, you most definitely not going to get laid now, playboy.

"Aw, man. Run me by my house."

David and LaQuan delivered the food to happy faces. They moved through the house to the kitchen and noticed the place had filled with bodies of all shapes and shades of brown. They felt like heroes...Until David announced, "WE WOULD HAVE BEEN HERE SOONER BUT MY BOY PISSED HIS PANTS! I HAD TO TAKE HIM HOME TO CHANGE HIS PANTIES AND SLACKS."

"No, no. He lying," LaQuan blushed. "You a sell out, kid."

"Calm down. I ain't mentioned THAT YOU CRIED!" David moved out of the kitchen.

Over the laughter, the music caught David's attention. "What the hell is that y'all playing?"

"It ain't music," one dude said.

"It's time to do something about that music. Whitey been gone for an hour and he still playing Freddie Jackson's wack ass So So Def Christmas CD. White people don't like the fake Luther either."

David took the CD out and cracked it. "He searched through and filled the CD changer with updated jams, one Christmas CD and the rest dancing hits.

The first song came on and the crowd exhaled and suddenly there was a dance floor where the coffee table used to take up space.

"It's on and poppin'," David said.

"This is what I am talking about," the dude said, offering David a high--five. "This is how the party is supposed to be."

"I usually don't do the high-five thing, but since you love me, it's all right this one time."

"Heyyyy!" a large woman shouted; she came through the door dancing, coat and church hat still on. "Let's get this party thumpin'! Teddy gotta know we can still party hearty!"

It was LaNett Stanley. Verdie loved her as family; she was a cousin of Teddy's that lived near Macon. But Verdie hated how she would bring bottles of cheap wine and then her and husband would drink up Teddy's top shelf liquor all night/ Teddy never complain, it was part of the party, he'd say. She and her husband and kids drove up every year and they stayed the night. Brings in bottles of cheap wine even though she only drinks hard liquor.

"I got you girl!" Bebe shouted as loud as LaNett, "We sliding now!"

Oh, Bebe loved her some LaNett.

Bebe changed the music. Some folks complained until they heard she put on some Electric/Mississippi Slide music. The party people began to get in lines and it was on. The coordination was funky at first, but eventually people fell in step. Of course, there are a few out of step.

David ran out there and was dancing opposite of the crowd. People laughed at him.

"What you doing, fool?" LaQuan asked, laughing.

"I'm doing Georgia, they doing Mississippi. They corn-fused. Why don't you come on out here? Can't keep no rhythm?"

"Nah, fool. That's that sissy dance. Only mens you see doing that is Cowboys and sissy. And I ain't got no horse."

"Or no girlfriend, yee-haw!"

Grandmomma shoved LaQuan toward the dance floor, "If that's the case, you should be out there then, sissy."

The people within earshot hooted and hollered in laughter. LaQuan got upset. "I'ma tell you one mo' 'gen."

Grandmomma sat back down, and licked her fingers, "Tell me again. Sucker."

"I ain't no sissy, you should know that."

"You sound like one right there."

David noticed Ginata's awesome smile. For the first time he felt something while looking at her. He reached out for her, "Come, girl."

She blushed and shook her head no. David broke through the ranks and begins dancing conventionally for his girl. She likes how he moves.

Marc didn't like the dance. "No, I am with LaQuan on this one. I don't do that."

"Do it for me," Patricia said softly, batting her eyes.

"Okay, let's do it."

"Sellout," LaQuan shouted.

Verdie stood at the edge of the dancing. She loved that her living room has become a dance floor; everyone, even the folks not dancing, were smiling. She pictured her husband loving the sight. Teddy would have done this sooner, she was thinking. He sure knew how to party. She felt warm, and her arms goose bumped under her dress's sleeves. She fought tears and they won, her hands wiped them away.

"Ma, come on!" David said.

She laughed and didn't know why.

And then her other son took her out there, Adam led her by her waist and got her in the groove.

Verdie saw her mother trying to get up. "Get momma," she told Adam. He went but she was trying to get to the CD player.

"Put some *Dramatics*, some *Chi-Lites* on. You ain't got no *Brook Benton*?"

"You gonna dance?"

"Put some *Al Green* on and you'll see some dancing. You got to have some music so I can dance up on somebody."

"That's next, Grandmomma. You know how it goes."

People are set now to eat and dance the night away.

David stepped off the dance floor, assuring Ginata he'd be back.

"Where you going, fool?"

"I need to chill for a minute."

"Chill?"

"I gotta take a dump, if you must know."

"Do that, I need to get my eat on."

David heads for steps, to use his mother's bathroom upstairs. A cousin that was never friendly, then became a crack head and now walks with the Lord caught David before the first step up.

"David, young brother, are you coming back to the Lord? He knows your pain."

"Oh, yeah, I'm coming back. I got some shit to do first. I'll holla."

His cousin frowned.

27

Rev. Penny had eyes only for BeBe. She caught him staring and shook her head blushing.

Before Penny became a minister he had a serious history with Bebe. It began at the first Christmas party. He was introduced to Verdie's sister and he was in love. They even made love that night, well it was love in his eyes.

Verdie liked the Reverend. She thought he was a cutie but away from the party he was a dud. He lacked the gift of gab and tried to hard to be cool.

And, Bebe never played down or got over getting caught on tape making out with Penny.

Now, the Reverend was single again; his wife left him for a usher in the church he took over. It was scandalous, but the fact that he was sleeping with a few of his congregation softened the blow. Rev. Penny would love another chance to make Bebe, who never married, his woman.

He was pushing up pretty hard, and Bebe was holding him off easily.

"I just want a kiss for old time's sake," the Rev begged.

"Then why we gotta go upstairs to do it?"

"That was how we did it in the old times."

"You ain't just trying to kiss my lips."

"Honey dip, I'll kiss whatever you need kissing. Tongue and all."

"You a mess, now stop. You a man of the cloth."

"These cloths is missing you, honey bunny."

"Shut up."

David was in relax mode on the toilet; dreaming about ending the night naked with Yvette in the bed with him. Those lips, wow.

Then the door busted open and his aunt and the good Reverend Penny were in the bathroom with him.

The Reverend said, "Jesus the son."

"That's me. Now close the door. I am not finished yet."

They left giggling.

"All them girls downstairs and he up here, jiggling with himself," the Reverend said.

"Was he playing with himself?" Bebe wondered.

"Hey!" David yelled. "Ain't y'all a little too old to ridicule a man doing something natural?"

David came downstairs and was feeling ten pounds lighter.

"I thought you fell in," LaQuan said.

"Had your girl on my lap."

"Right."

David nodded and followed.

They found a set of double parked cars a few feet from the house, in the dark away from the streetlights, and fired up some weed. They smoked and hid the blunt well, while talking about nothing important. It wasn't long before Adam, the master of smoking for free, joined them.

"Don't hide, divide."

"Why don't you dig in your pockets and put something on this."

LaQuan offered the lumpy blunt, hiding it from view in the palm of his hand.

"I don't support other people's habit. I only do a drag or two, that don't cost nothing."

"Keep telling yourself that."

"You sound like a damn addict."

"You young boys don't know how to pay homage."

"Why don't you pay money and stop smoking up people's shit."

Adam enjoyed a few hits. "You guys need better weed. You are not getting mellow. You smoking and still hating."

"Shut up," David said.

Adam chuckled and handed his brother the blunt. "The party is coming out right."

David took a long drag. "Yes, sir," he said without breathing.

"Puff puff pass," LaQuan complained. "You fools talking too much. Like y'all sisters."

"Don't mess up my high, please." David said.

Adam stood off the car. "You know what?"

"What?" David asked.

"I am going to something fun and be happy."

"Well, do that."

LaQuan passed the blunt to Adam, "Happy means gay."

Before Adam hit it he said, "A homo would know."

"Please. On that fact of wrong, I am going back in because I gots me a wife in there."

David scoffed, "You brought your blow up doll to my house for a sleep over again?"

Adam laughed. The blunt was now the size of a finger tip. "Finish this," he told David.

"No thanks."

Adam dragged it three strong, quick times and then put it out and pocketed it. They moved back to the house.

"Dave, hold up."

"Here."

David looked down and saw Adam had a CD. He took it and shook his head. "The damn Kurtis Blow CD."

"Yeah," he patted David's back. "You might need that."

"Asshole."

They walk in to a slow song and couples dragging.

Ginata and Caren were having fun hating on the folks at the party that were, in their eyes, fashionably challenged.

A woman passed them rocking a short dress and long hairdo.

"That ain't BeBe," Caren frowned. "Those BBs on her dress stand for Broke and Busted."

Ginata shook her head, "That's a Glamour don't, with her Sushi bag and Dontoffendme shoes."

Caren giggles. "And nice hair. No wonder there's a horse out there picketing."

"Oh my God, how come buddy over there got his momma's sweater on?"

"Aw. He thought since it was green and red it would be cool for Christmas."

"But it has sequins!"

"Shame. He ain't gonna get laid wearing that."

They both couldn't help but notice the big smile LaQuan had looking their way.

"What he smiling for like that?" Caren asked.

"He ignorant as hell and don't know any better."

Caren laughed, and LaQuan noticed how her face lit up when she showed happiness.

"He's cute, though," Ginata told Caren. "But he could use some maintenance and a ton of common sense."

"He needs to stop letting his mother dress him."

"Oh, Lord," Ginata shook her head. "Why he coming over here?"

"Hey, now," LaQuan said.

"Hey," Caren replied.

"Y'all was talking about me?"

"You work with Ginata, right? And you David's best friend?"

"That's right. And so you know me. So just go ahead and start making out."

"Ah, no."

Ginata couldn't stop laughing.

"Wait," Caren shifted and pointed at LaQuan, he smiled at the attention. "Ain't you the guy that ran out of gas and had to walk a mile home to ask your momma for five dollars?

"So what that mean? Why you bring that up?"

Ginata shook her head and folded her arms. *Damn he stupid*, she was thinking. "Just to let my girl now what's up."

"What? 'Cause I live with my mother? I stay with my momma 'cause I don't see a reason to have my own place.

Ginata and her friend laughs.

"Right. What about when you get married?"

LaQuan replied, his right hand on his chest, fingers wide, "Who? Me? Ah, hell nah. I ain't getting married. You ain't hear me? I already got my momma talking mess.

"You special," Caren said.

"Whoops," Ginata sat up, "there goes my date. See y'all."

Caren laughed. "Go and conquer, girlie."

Ginata cut between the three men and took David's hand and without a word led him into the middle of the dance floor.

"Dang girl, what you a cavewoman or something?"

She slid close into his body and got him into the rhythm of the song.

"I like this," David said.

"Good. I want you to." She smiled and rested her head on his shoulder.

"You notice how nice I am being? My hand is on your back, I could, you know, slip it down a little, because that is nice down there, but I ain't even going there."

"You are not being nice. You just know better."

Patricia swayed to the oldie but goodie; someone had found his dad's *Blue Magic* CD and the group slowed the party down. She was watching David dance. "They make a nice couple," she said to Marc, sitting next to her. He nodded.

"Dance with me."

Patricia puts her drink down, "Sure."

Grandmomma wanted to dance. This was here kind of groove. She threw a cup cake toward LaQuan and hit Horace Brown. Horace was pissed until he saw that it was his grandmother. He was a forty-something year old thug, a cousin on Verdie's side of the family. He is sitting with his two girlfriends, neither looked over seventeen.

"Get that fool next to you," she said.

Horace tapped LaQuan and smirked at the fear in LaQuan's eyes. "Yo, Grandmomma wants you."

"For real?" LaQuan looked over there and she was waving for him.

He came over and Grandmomma stood up. "Come on and let's dance."

"Aw hell naw. No bets. Last year you was too nasty, granny."

"Sissy. Go on from here then. Go cry about."

LaQuan went back to his spot. He liked sitting over there where he and Wallace were the only men in a group of females that had taken over a corner of the living room.

He decided to talk to David while he was dancing with Ginata.

"Hey, Dave, y'all got that new Tupac Christmas album?"

"Of course."

"Is it hittin' on anything?"

LaQuan cut in, "That joker snapping. Him and Lil Jon on their doing chestnuts roasting. Off the ball *and* chain."

The folks around them laughed, except Wallace and his pretty young dates.

"It's got some nice beats," David said.

"But it's stupid, to hear buddy talking angry and stuff. Talkin' about killing folks that are still alive and making money."

"Like he is," one of the pretty young girls with Wallace said.

"Aw, hell naw. You think he still alive when he dead as hell?"

People laughed except Wallace and them girls.

"That is not funny. He is no one to laugh at. Tupac died for our sins and has come back to lead us down the righteous path to glory."

"You crazy, shorty."

"Don't call my girl crazy," Wallace said.

"My bad, I was just sayin'..." before LaQuan could take back his statement the girl jumped up. She stood over LaQuan, with both fists clinched tightly, and snapped, "That's our savior you laughing at, don't get cut up."

"Whoa, baby girl. Yo, player, get your girl?"

Wallace sat back, "She alright," he said.

She told LaQuan, "Tupac was a prophet that the white man did not respect."

"Okay, right, right."

David, hiding his laugh, said, "Damn, player, you get women excited for real."

28

Karl had been watching his sister in law for most of the time he and his wife were at the party. Verdie had told him she didn't want to talk that night but he was determined to catch her alone.

His eyes followed her still shapely body head for the steps up to the bedrooms and he sprang up, telling his wife he would be right back.

Verdie had gone to share some of her left over gift wrap from her bedroom. She entered her room and didn't see or feel that Karl was right behind her and in the doorway.

"Miss Verdie," he said softly.

Still she was startled.

"Karl, what are you doing up here?"

He respected her personal space still he slowly drifted into the room. "Verdie, baby. We need to dialogue about this money situation."

"Dialogue? About what money? Karl, how many times I have to tell you there's nothing left behind for you or his sister."

"I am supposed to believe that?"

"That's just the way it is. It's nothing to do with fair."

"I mean, I respected you all this time. I never went the legal route or nothing like that. I just want what's coming to me.

"What money do you think my husband had? He had no real job."

"Yeah, but he had real money. He told me so himself, told me what I was to get."

"When was this, in a dream?"

"You making jokes? Where is it? What you do with it?

Verdie sighed. "My husband didn't like you. If he had left money for his sister, she would have gotten it."

Karl shook his head. "Maybe you kept it."

"Karl, whatever. You are here, enjoy yourself, but leave me alone about some damn money."

"All your kids got new cars and shit. You done moved your momma here. You think we all fools."

"To hell with you, Karl."

She moved to pass him and he grabbed hold of her arm.

"Get your hands off me."

"You are not going to just walk by me and disrespect me."

Patricia moved into the room and sets a scare into both of them. Verdie wriggled free and left them for her bathroom. With the door closed they heard her cry.

"What did you do to my momma."

"You mean what has she been busted doing to others." Karl walked out.

Patricia followed him all the way down to the living room.

He sat with his wife. Patricia stood over them.

"What did you say to my mother?"

"The truth. And she couldn't handle it. Your father was disrespectful."

"The truth? What truth?" Patricia voice rose to the decibel of the party's music. People were sliding to an R. Kelly song.

David heard his sister voice and although he couldn't tell what she was saying he knew right off she was annoyed. He looked to see she was talking to Uncle Karl and then he knew what was up.

"Y'all think y'all can screw us out of ours, you're wrong. Dead wrong."

"You are going to apologize to my mother or you have to leave."

"What did you do to momma?"

David was there now.

Karl stood. "Your father was disrespectful to me and that ain't got nothing to do with the money he left his sister."

"Look how you treated his sister," David said.

More people looked then; from the dance floor and among the party people, most every eye was on them.

"Auntie wouldn't let dad bust your ass. So you don't really know how dad felt about you."

"What goes on in my house ain't none of nobody's business but ours. You father was an bastard long before that.

"Same here," Patricia said.

David said, "You got what you were getting from daddy. So knock it off or be out."

Verdie came quickly. "David, it's okay, baby. Calm down. I'm alright."

"Bunk that. If pops wanted him to have a slice he would have cut it for him and put his name on it."

"Y'all are all foul. Just like he was!"

People slowed their dancing; looking in the direction of the complaining man.

"Then what are you doing here, then?" Patricia challenged.

"He's gone. Thank God. That is why I felt like I could come here."

"Get the fuck out."

Now the party was silent but the music. Not many of the people there that knew Patricia had ever heard her curse.

David moved through the crowd and got their coats. He came back and Karl was still talking junk.

David said, "Auntie, you don't have to leave."

She just glared at David. She had to side with her husband, her expression held.

Karl reached to snatch the coats and David moved them.

"Ain't you got manners?"

Auntie Mary gently took the coats from David. "Enough, okay?"

"Yes ma'am."

"You chubby punk!"

"Karl, that's enough," Auntie Mary said. She led Karl out the door.

29

Yvette Paulding parked on the street of the Taylor home behind a long row of SUVs and cars.

She used to live on the block, right there in the big, Victorian house, next to the Taylor's. She had been in their house as much as hers. She was an only child and they were like her cousins, and often times like her own brothers and sisters.

As usual, the house was crowded to bursting with their "intimate" friends of the moment. She saw a family member she remembered arguing at many Taylor parties leaving in a huff.

"I should go get my gun," Karl barked through the night."

"Just hush," his wife said.

Just like old times, Yvette smiled.

From the house she heard the noise of party people. Christmas carols blared from the stereo Teddy was so proud of, voices were raised as people shouted to one another from room to room, and at least a half-dozen children ran around, seemingly in circles, screaming excitedly.

All in all, Yvette mused, even with the master of ceremonies passed away, it was the same old general mess. She had decided right away that she wasn't going to go in. She took out her cell phone and found Pooh Bear, her name for David. She pressed, and with a smile waited for him to answer, sure that despite the noise and whatever he might be into, he'd answer her call.

David's cell vibrated in his pocket. And he knew right away it was his Boo. He moved away from his boy and answered it. LaQuan tried to speak with a hot girl, brought to the party by some of David's Macon cousins.

"What you driving?" the brown-skinned, thick honey said.

"A car, what you think?"

She threw up her hand, "Poof, be gone."

LaQuan came to David. "She wants me, dude."

"Nice."

Ginata, across the room, on the couch couldn't help staring; she was searching his eyes, his demeanor for a sign that his girl wasn't coming.

David hung up.

"That was your kissing cousin?"

"My date is coming. You need me to help you blow up yours?"

"I don't bring crabs to the sea, player."

"What? You are so damn unsmart. It's fish to the sea; sand to the beach. No, crabs is what your cousin gave you in middle school when you boned her.

"I'll be right back. Don't do nothing stupid until I get back to witness it."

"Go on with your whipped ass. You supposed to turn that around. You supposed to whip the pussy!"

Older folks looked at LaQuan with disapproval.

"Sorry. Talking about his cat."

David searched the night and spots Yvette's Honda idling across the street. The tinted window rolled down and revealed her round, soft face. She waved him over.

He jogged to her. "What's up, you not coming in?"

"How's it going in there?"

"It's going alright. I mean, it's just not the same this year. We all knew that. But it's definitely not the same without you. Are you coming in or what?

"I have to talk to you. Get in." She watched him walk around and pull her door open. He got into her ride. A mellow love song played as she cut the engine. David leaned in for a kiss and Yvette acted stunned with the gesture. She didn't respond or even move to accommodate him.

"What's up?" David backed away, sensing something was wrong. "Damn, is my breath that bad?"

"No, it's not that...Look, David. What are we doing?"

"What do you mean what are we doing?"

"Us, this relationship. Why did we choose to walk down this path together?"

"Because we know each other better than anyone. Because you know what's in my heart."

"True that. That's the reason we've been friends all these years, David. That has nothing to do with a committed relationship...When your Dad died in August, it hurt me a lot. But I was hurt more for the pain that you must have been feeling behind that. I was worried about you. I couldn't bare to see you like that. And I was willing to do anything to ease that pain just a little...even make love to you. But you're a strong person, David. You've always been. I've always known that."

"So, what you saying?"

"That we should stay friends."

"Stay friends?"

"We should move to that next level, I mean."

"You saying what we did, it was sympathy sex? You felt sorry for me?"

"No, no. I felt what you felt. But now it's not about us being physical."

She puts her hand over his.

"So what now? You kicking me to the curb?"

"Don't say it like that."

"What is it? I have been wanting forever to be your man."

"I know," her eyes stayed on his. "I know. But I am seeing Bruce. He is my boyfriend."

"So what, what we did? Just fucked?"

No. I mean, yes but it was between friends, something right."

"Shit, I was thinking it was something right different. You been fucking with that fool for how long? He don't care about you."

"I love you, Dave. Always."

He sighed.

"I bought you something for Christmas."

"Give it to that nigger Bruce."

"So you mad?"

"Dogs get mad."

Yvette nodded her understanding. Their eyes met.

"So, me," he said, "I got it all wrong?"

"I love you, have all my life."

"But."

"But Bruce I am in love with."

"He's a drummer in a girl band."

"Be nice."

"I am tired of being nice. I mean, shit, he is a drummer for a girl band, what?"

Yvette sighed. "You being mean is making it easier to dump you."

"Good. Then you can go on."

They sat in silence a moment.

He didn't want to get out but he didn't want to be around her. And she wanted him to forever be that friend she had always had to lean on.

She said, "David, we're more than this relationship was. I remember the first thing you said to me in kindergarten. You said, 'Can I sit next to you?' Damn that the teacher had assigned seats."

David nodded, "And you said, 'why you want to sit here?' all sassy n' stuff. Little bad ass."

"And you said - 'because you're pretty.'"

They laughed at the memory.

"Yup, you were definitely a cutie back then. But now you just fell off."

She pinched him. "Asshole. Take that back."

"We cool?" she asked.

"Yeah, fuck it, we cool. Forever. We go back like bucket seats."

She smiled.

"But you still not coming in? Your momma is in there dancing with everybody like she single."

"Shut up. No. I'm not coming in. Going out."

"With the girl drummer."

"Dave?"

"Sorry."

"Hey...since you say we cool and all that," Yvette's voice livened. "If we were still, you know, friendly, can I get a booty call every now and again?"

"Yeah, I knew I put it on you. But ah, you can't get no more. What, you think I'm like Quan. You can just dump me and still get some?"

"Can't blame a sister for askin'."

"Naw, I don't blame you. I'll miss it but we should just let that go."

"Okay, okay...Then hit the next girl hard and long for me.

"Oh, for sure. I can do that."

"Bye."

David moved in for a hug and she caressed him.

She started the car and he got out. She waved and she was gone.

David looked up at the night sky, full of stars, and wondered how could he have thought it was more to them than the excellent sex? What a fool he was, he considered,

It was dead, though. The love, or infatuation, or whatever it was that David had felt for Yvette was suddenly completely dead; Yvette had killed it as easily as it had grow in him for years. That was how she wanted it, over with, so cool, he thought.

David took a deep breath. Fuck it was his attitude. He turned his head back into the house.

Walking with his head down, David didn't see that Ginata was standing on the porch. She spoke when he got close.

"You okay?"

"Yeah, I'm cool."

"She's not coming in?"

"No, she's got things to do."

"Too bad for her. It's a nice party."

Ginata makes her move. She had watched him closely with Yvette, and she sense that he had been dumped by a female he should not have respected and given so much love to, she felt.

"I'm trying to spend the party with you."

"What's up with you and the cripple?"

"Meanie!"

He laughed.

"He is not my date, he is my friend. Like you, But I want you to be more than that. Always have."

"What? Really?"

"Yes."

"Well, let's kill the talking for now. We got some Chinese food. And then, how about we agitate the rug?"

"I'm with that."

"And then later, I got my own room in this joint."

"Ah, no. We have to work toward that."

"Oh, you a lady, huh?"

"For sure. But when it comes time to be up and naked, there won't be no lady around to help save you."

"My damn!"

30

David felt very ready to deliver the speech.

Everybody was happy; aided by the heavy-handed punch David had made.

He moved to the stereo and rigged up his dad's 1980s microphone to the stereo. Some people were watching, not exactly knowing what he was up to, but his brother did. The toast was to be the big moment of the night. And Adam was immediately disturbed that his brother was stepping up to do it. First of all, Adam felt as the oldest it was his right, and secondly he just knew his brother was going to mess it up.

Adam moved to intercept his brother. "What are you doing?"

"Frying eggs. What it look like?"

"Ha. But you are not getting ready to make the toast of the night. I've worked too hard for this and you-"

"Damn, calm down, man. I'm just the opening act. Just let me say my peace. You can have the mic after I rock it. Besides, ain't all your white people gone?"

Adam stood away, bitter, while David took center stage in the room. He caught the glare from his mother. He saw that she knew he was hating on his brother and that she wanted this for her baby boy in her pleading eyes. He cursed before softening; shit, he thought, this ain't my party and it ain't his either.

David went to tapping a glass.

"Hello...testing..." was how David began. His voice is loud and clear in the room. Everyone mingling and mixing turned toward him. Verdie and Patricia came in from the dining room. Grandmomma, LaQuan, Marc and all the others looked on. Rev Penny and BeBe stand near the tree, the Reverend took the chance while everyone's eyes were elsewhere to get a good look at Bebe's body.

"Lord have the mercy."

"Yes, right?" Bebe responded.

"It is right. Yes it is."

"Ah, excuse me folks. Well, this is my first time doing the toast. I'm really up here introducing my brother Adam and his thing, but I just wanted to say a few words first...I, um..."

David looked out among all the people and gets even more nervous; especially when he saw the sparkle in Ginata's eyes amongst the crowd. She stared at him with anticipation, giving him a smile.

"...You know, this party is about a boy from, or a family from the south side of Chicago. They lived in the projects and every year at Christmas time they would...they would gather, because they were hungry. I mean, they didn't have much to eat because they were poor. And so they played music and danced on Christmas Eve...and this got them through a lot...I mean, this meant a lot to them..."

"What in God's name of hell is he talking about," the man in the wheelchair said too loudly.

Verdie looked on, concerned. "Take your time, baby."

Adam looked down, ashamed for his brother's failure. And he looked up, willing David to pull it off, to comeback and finish strong.

"Go ahead, man you got it," LaQuan said.

And Adam felt ashamed for himself that he hadn't tossed out words of encouragement.

"...Because the holidays is a time for people to come together and celebrate..." He was reading what he wrote as if he had never seen the handwriting before. "...being together."

David looked up, he was getting hot, and the street caught his eye, his attention, the star on top, then the blinking lights, and then the Reverend's head turned licking his lips at the sight of his aunt's breasts.

He swallowed, trying to get his might right, He looked back at his prepared speech and started in again, damned because he didn't know where he had left off.

"...Christmas is not just about baby Jesus and Santa Claus, it's about giving and receiving presents and music and not always getting the present you wanted because the person giving it to you was too cheap or didn't care enough to put out the extra loot and..."

People were staring at him like he was speaking in Hebrew.

His mother had a blank stare, seemingly not really looking at her son bomb. Patricia smiled and nodded, when they caught eyes, trying to be encouraging. But when he looked at his brother, Adam was smirking with his arms folded across his chest, and shook his head in mock.

LaQuan can't stand to see his boy struggling like this. He looks away; scratching his head.

David took a deep breath. "So, I mean, I was saying, after a while...this family...which was my father's family if ya'll didn't catch that before...became so popular with their Christmas party, people came from miles around to sing and dance."

Grandmomma said, "That boy is perspiring worst than a South Carolina slave at harvest,"

Reading his words he began to feel as though he wasn't making sense. He wasn't, he was sure, and he couldn't get himself to go on. His body heated and his mouth went dry. He was sweating like it was August in Atlanta instead of Christmas time.

"...ah damn. I don't know what the hell I'm doing up here...Fuck."

"Ha ha," one of his cousins mocked him like the bully on *The Simpsons*.

He moved through the crowd and heard a few giggles and whispers.

Then his homeboy yelled out, "Go, playboy," LaQuan had a hand at his mouth to hid his laugh, "but you still my man, a hundred grand."

LaQuan turned to the next man and said, "My man, he my man, but he was downright awful."

"Shut up," Ginata said, her arms folded and a foot bouncing from crossed legs.

31

David was sitting at the base of the front steps with his head in his hands. The front door fly's open and Rev Penny comes running and slipping out and screaming about the devil. David looks at him curiously as Penny disappears down the street.

He looked up to the night sky and let's out a deep breath. He silently apologized to his dad above for fucking up his traditional speech. And for the party being so screwy.

"Dave, yo, what you doing."

The sudden voice startled him. Then Adam sat next to him.

"What's up? You can't borrow no money, pimpin'."

"Funny," Adam punched him in the arm, "Where that fifty you owe me, *pimpin'*."

"This ain't about me."

"Baby bro', your speech wasn't that bad."

"I stunk. It was ridiculous," David was shaking his head.

"No way was it ridiculous," Adam clapped him on his back. "It was from your heart."

"Naw, I know I messed that up."

"At least you went there. Speaking in front of a crowd at easy, especially these folks that had been drinking."

"I don't know. It was like all I wrote down didn't make any sense. And then I saw Mommy looking right at me. It was like bang, I didn't even know why I was up there."

"Yeah, dad used to keep it nice and short, sweet and to the point. And then end it with a joke about them being greedy; eating and drinking up all his shit once a year."

David nodded. He looked at his brother and noticed Adam seemed more relaxed than usual and hoped that his brother hadn't let the night defeat him.

"Look, I'm sorry you didn't get your deal but on the real, I am also happy in a way." David had Adam's attention and he continued by saying, "Dad never trusted that cracker."

Adam just nodded. He had been so focused on his hunt for money, power and respect to see that his dad would not have approved of his connection with Dan Sweeney.

"Bunk that deal. Like dad would say, if it was meant to be another somebody better will come along and do me better."

"True, true. You gonna be alright."

"You really think you need the white vote to win Atlanta?"

"I do. You don't think so?"

"No. Not after what happen to the last sellout. He in jail, they sold him out."

"I ain't gonna let that shit happen."

"That's what he said. Look, we outnumber them in the city. Me, I would do like Marion Berry did for years in D.C."

"Weed is about as bad as I get."

"No. Not smoke crack and bang nasty women," David laughed, "He won by getting out there and getting people a) interested in voting and 2) a way and a means to there to vote. Damn that MARTA bus system. You gotta go get them."

"Hmmm," Adam pondered the idea.

"Election day I'd turn this city into a big party.

"Our people party too much as it is."

"Never that. We got things to forget. To get away from. You in the city politics already, work with somebody, open some doors. Get jobs, find jobs. That's the key. Money, you gotta keep it rolling."

"Oh, excuse me. I didn't know it was that easy. I can just pluck jobs off a tree."

"Nothing is easy, fool. But that is what people are worried about, paying bills and living well enough to relax. To have Time to see their kids grow.

"So I am an asshole for hanging with whitey? A sellout?"

"It's about what you feel. I ain't right, but it's how I feel. It's about where your heart is."

"Where's your heart?"

David stands straight.

"I love you for asking me that. Finally."

"Really?" Adam sobered.

"My heart. I am opening my own business. I put my little money aside, gathered info, and in January I will be ready to open my music store, right downtown. I pick up the keys next week."

"Oh, okay. So you was on some double secret shit, couldn't tell anybody?"

"You see. I didn't have to go talk about like Negroes do. I was about it. No talk."

"Okay."

"That's what I did with my money."

Adam nodded. "I feel you, okay, relax."

"You didn't relax dogging me out about what I did with my money."

"Point taken."

"Look man, forget being real for awhile. Have some fun. Loosen your tie, congressman."

Adam grinned and shook his head, "Asshole.

"Dad wanted us to be someone. Professional, money makers, providers, lovers. All that."

"True, true."

"But what you seemed to have forgotten in all that was that he wanted us to have fun. To live life to the fullest."

"You high."

"Oh yes sir. High, yes. But that's my point. I'm doing what I want to do. At my family's home, with my brother, and my family all around. This is love. Enjoyment. Kid, this is how I want to live. Live how you want to live, but player, be happy."

"You right. And I know, man, Mom needed you here. It was better that you were here. I mean, she needed somebody here day in and day night."

"Nuff said, baby brother."

In a window of the house, Verdie had been watching and her eyes well with tears; tears of happiness.

32

David came back into the house to a roar of hilarity.

People were giggling, eyes closed in tears with LaQuan talking to them. David was not shocked and knew they were laughing at, not with, his boy. LaQuan was funny like that, and could do that to a group of people by just saying the wrong word at the right time.

David lost the conversation, though, he was taken aback by the sight of his mother's head thrown back in laughter. She was over there talking to her sister, and having a good time. He watched her for a moment, and the sight warmed his soul.

Then he heard his sister say, "David, tell them about when Quan used to date that retarded girl."

David tried to hide his laugh with a hand.

"What?" Ginata giggled.

"She wasn't retarded," LaQuan barked. "Y'all silly as hell." The laughter and attention was making LaQuan uneasy. "She just had a little of that Down Syndrome."

"A little?" Ginata was laughing to hard to speak.

Patricia finished the thought, "How do you have a little Down Syndrome?"

"Whatever. Y'all gonna fall off me."

David finally spoke, "Pimpin', you gotta admit that girl wasn't right in the head."

"And that's why she liked him," Patricia said.

"Fall off me, now."

"She is a rugby player in Ireland now, right?"

LaQuan hissed, "Aw, you liked her too, playboy. You said she had a big ass."

"I said that? Hold up, I was the one that was scared of her, man."

Grandmomma couldn't stay out of this one. She was nearby, eating hearty helpings of food, she said, "He dates retarded girls and he is a sissy. That boy is a mess."

Verdie called over to David through the noise. She and Bebe had been talking about the way he had doted after the young lady he worked with. She said, "You let her taste your chocolates?"

"Whoa. Momma?" David leaned back, hand on his chest in mock shock. "In front of everybody? I was going to wait until the afterparty."

"David! Always gotta be a joker."

The people around him laughed, except Ginata. She caught eyes with her friend Caren, who had her eyes raised.

David said, "Oh you mean the candy?"

Verdie shook her head, "Be nice."

"I am always nice, momma."

Ginata liked that he was smiling again, back to his old playful self.

Verdie said, "He made the brownie teddy bears, rocky road, chocolate pecan fudge."

"Really now. I didn't know you can bake."

"Oh, I'm helpful around the kitchen. It's in the bedroom, girl, that I am a mess. That's where I need help like a mug."

They all laughed again.

"Yeah," LaQuan quipped, "he sucks in the bed."

"Nice try. When you learn humor get back to us."

Ginata placed a hand on David's thigh to get his attention. She got it.

"Which of the brownies you made?"

He just stared at her, a sill grin on his face. David whispered, "You startin' something."

He was surprised that she didn't have a quip in response. Instead she looked back with an inviting smile. Her hand slid side to side.

"Your hand feels good."

She added caressing to the feeling of his leg.

"Get a room, dog," LaQuan said.

"Maybe soon," she said.

LaQuan froze in shock.

David lost his smile. "Come dance with me."

She got up and they embraced on the dance floor.

LaQuan shined a big smile at Caren. "What's up girl? Let's do this."

"Uh uh. I ain't no girl and you ain't grinding on me. No."

"You gay?"

"You stupid?"

"Yes he stupid," Grandmomma said. "Stupid, come put my plate in the trash."

"I ain't nobody's stupid," He took the plate and moved away.

Grandmomma got up and moved to the dance floor. She came up between David and Ginata. "Thank Jesus you not no sissy boy." She went into her purse. "Buy some condoms. The good kind."

"The good kind cost more than $5, Grandmomma."

"How you know?"

"Ha. Oh, I know."

"And come here, don't do it in the booty-hole. That's AIDS. And a sign you gay."

"Okay, Grandmomma. I'ma do it just natural."

Ginata grimaced, not believing she is hearing this conversation.

"And with a condom. Don't be like your cousin. Taking care of kids with no marriage papers. How he know they his?"

"That's what I am trying to wonder."

33

Reverend Penny watched the door to the bathroom with baited breath. He moved to it and put an open palm on it. He silently prayed.

The door opened and BeBe stepped out and was startled by the Rev standing right there.

"Look where we at, once again," the Reverend said. "I bet it smells like roses in there."

"You need to stop, None of that anymore."

"Ohh, you scared me? Good, I mean good because I is sooo scared of us again."

Bebe looked startled by him. But it's something more. He knows her. She returns the same gaze and for an instant their memories are intertwined.

"Lenny?"

"Beatrice?"

They both took deep breaths and recomposed themselves.

"I mean you are preacher now, we can't be just up in some bathroom."

"Yeah, uh, that's me. Reverend Penny is what they call me." He was looking her up and down, checking her out but caught himself.

"I'll, um, let you do your business in there and I'll see you when you get out."

"No, you are supposed to come in with me. You know? Like we was, like old times."

"No, that is not going to happen. We are too old for that."

"Well, then be with me, be with me afterwards, be with me always."

"You proposing?"

"I think?"

She smiled, "You think?" She ran a finger along his chin, "You just lusting right now, sinner."

The Reverend went into the bathroom and shut the door.

BeBe took a deep breath and left him to himself.

Alone, he cried out, "Get back, devil!" He knelt down on both knees praying over the toilet. "Oh, I know you testing me, you testing my will, Lord. You said the demon will always come with a smile and a nice round pair of...oh, Lord deliver me from temptation!"

He came out of the bathroom in tears. When reached the living room, Bebe intercepted him and took his hand.

"Come on and dance with me, fool."

34

Patricia had to get away.

Away from Marc's intense eyes, away from the fact that her first impulse was to talk to her father about it all; she just had to get away from the party for just a minute.

She went into the kitchen with the intention of stepping out onto the back porch to gather her emotions. She didn't have to say yes right now, no. he was wrong for just popping the question on her.

Hadn't she seen it coming?

Patricia was at the back door but she hadn't gone out yet. She just stood there looking out to the woods, where when she was 12 her and her father went out on an adventure to see where the woods led. Her father promised they would see bears and tigers eating deer and rabbits. It gross her out, the thought of the carnage, but she stayed at his side.

They found nothing but a weak creek and the houses on the other side. Teddy said it was because they were talking, and thus had scared the wildlife away. "They thought we were hunters," he said.

Patricia sighed. She just wished she could ask her dad one question right then; *how do you know the right thing to do?*

She had asked him that before, and she recalled his answer, *it's what you think is right. And then you deal with the consequences.*

"Smart, Daddy. Real smart to leave it up to me," she smiled and shook her head. She knew, deep down. She can't hide from the topic.

"What's that now?" Verdie asked.

"Oh, I thought I was alone, just talking to myself."

"Don't do that. Sign of crazy."

"Marc proposed to me tonight."

Verdie stopped moving. Her eyes searched her daughter's hands, both.

"And?" Verdie asked anxiously.

"And. I don't know."

"Is that what you told him?"

Patricia looked away, back out the window. "I - it's just that this is unchartered territory for me. You know how Dad was with any man that came within six feet of me."

"And you can't see that that's your problem now? That you never had the responsibility of making your own choice about a man because Ted was here for that. Now that he's not here, you have to make that decision for yourself."

"I don't know what to do, what to say. I don't know where to start."

Verdie put her hand on Patricia's chest. "Start right here. What it tells you to do, do. And stand behind the decision. Honey," Verdie sighed, "It's the grown up thing to do, and you have been a grown up a long while. So, just be you."

Patricia let the words absorb.

Verdie hugged her. And then her mother was gone. Patricia was alone again.

Her mother didn't even ask her if she loved Marc.

Patricia asked herself. And the answer didn't come. All that came was a montage of Marc loving her, caring for her and being gentle with her. She loved the feeling he gave her when they were alone, was her answer.

After a minute or so, Patricia decided to rejoin the party. She had no decision, only to let things happen, whatever that meant. She basically was going to wait for him to ask again, and go for there. Part coward, part patient and full of shit, she knew but she had no other feeling on the matter.

She walked back to the spacious living room that no longer had breathing space. Everybody was on the dance floor; either standing watching or slow dancing to a love song.

Perfect, Patricia thought.

She saw that her aunt was out there, dancing with someone she couldn't see, they turn, gliding, and it was LaQuan. My God, was Patricia's reaction, she laughed. Bebe caught her eyes. "I like me a dumb one," she said to Patricia. "That's right," LaQuan replied, his head rested on her breasts. Her brothers were out there grinding; Adam with his wife and David with a co-worker, and David seemed serious.

She looked for Marc and found that he was looking at her. He had a blank look on his face. He moved to her and her feet turned to cement.

"Come dance with me," he said, taking her by the hand.

He got her into the groove and when she looked up to him he kissed her.

But he didn't ask again.

35

David walked Ginata and her friends to her car.

He helped the disabled guy into the mini SUV, and then he broke down the chair and put it in the back. Caren hugged him and she got in the back seat.

David and Ginata were alone in the dark evening.

"So, did you have a good time?"

"Yes, it was interesting."

"Don't lie. This was one of the worst Taylor Christmas parties ever. Trust me. But it was interesting for sure."

"So, is everything still on point with the store?"

"Yup. Three more weeks till opening day."

"So that's three more weeks of working together."

"Three more weeks of mixing business with pleasure. Which reminds me, we're breaking your little policy now."

"No we're not. Breaking the policy would be you grabbing me around my waist and kissing me."

And what's the punishment for such a violation?"

"Withholding of your wages. Immediate termination."

"Hmm, let me think about that one..."

He took a step toward her.

"Maybe I'll just quit now, and then you can quit and come work for me. And then there can be a new policy."

"Maybe..."

"David. I want a kiss."

"You know you can get what you want."

He kissed her eyelids and the corners of her mouth, delighting when they turned up with pure pleasure. And then his whole focus centered on her mouth, and she opened to him as a flower being worshipped by the sun.

David outlined her lips with the tip of his tongue. When her tongue touched his, a tremor of need made her throat and breast quiver.

Ginata got more than she bargained for. She planted her hand in his chest, "We need to stop."

"Get rid of the dead weight and come back here. We can get to know each other better."

"You are a mess, Dave. Good night. We'll talk tomorrow, when you are nice and sober."

"You want to go out with me?"

"Huh? Yeah. I want to."

"I mean, you know, dating. I want to see you."

"Ain't a damn thing wrong with that."

36

As the night winded down, Verdie allowed herself to remember a good past, filled with marvelous memories of great people, memories of zany moments and loving times.

People were yelling back as they left, telling Verdie they have had a great time. She proudly waved them away.

She carried two glasses of Egg Nog into the living room. She hands one to her mother. She oversees her family. Everybody was relaxing.

Bebe, her feet up on the coffee table, said, "See, it turned out just fine. Everybody's having a good time."

"True. It was nice."

"Well, almost everybody. There's some white folks that won't be looking forward to next year's party.

"That's true. And too bad for them."

Verdie heard her youngest was seeing out a few stragglers.

"Now that was what I call a party!"

"What y'all niggers doing for New Year's Eve?"

"Not a damn thing, so don't come by here and good night!"

"David!" Verdie scolded.

Verdie moved on and as she hit the living room her eyes did a quick scan.

LaQuan is in and out of a drunken sleep. Bebe has a glass of wine with the bottle between her legs. Grandmomma sips Egg Nog. Marc and Patricia were close, in separate chairs, whispering.

Grandmomma said, "It ain't enough rum in this. That's why nobody drank any."

Verdie sat in her favorite chair and allowed relaxation to seep in. Right then, for the first time that night, she missed her husband so.

And then she thought soon it would be just her. All of a sudden she felt alone. Her mind went through the nightmarish images of her children all getting married and living their lives, with her growing old alone. Alone was how she felt all of a sudden; and all alone in the world after always being in a full house all her life. She was raised with six brothers and sisters, and after she married Teddy they had lived with her sister and her four kids in a three-bedroom ranch house for two long years.

Oh how Teddy would have been pissed about how the party went. But he would have liked how it ended.

She then felt bad that she had fought since Thanksgiving to not have this party, an event she so enjoyed.

The sensation hurt. She coughed out a cry and fought away sobs. Still a soft smile curved Verdie's face. She wiped her face, praying no one noticed.

She wanted everyone to stay the night, sleep wherever, or not to sleep, and she would cook breakfast.

"You okay, V?" BeBe asked after a sip of her wine, her feet up on the coffee table. "What's so funny? I thought you were crying."

David came back in as the last few people file out. The core family is all that remains. Adam, BeBe, Patricia, Grandmomma, Mardessa, Marc and Verdie were seated around the living room.

David plopped down next to his boy; no one else dared to sit next to LaQuan. "Ooooh we. We done."

Patricia got up. "Well, I am going to start on the kitchen."

"No," Verdie protested. "Sit a spell."

"I don't know how much longer we are going to stay."

On that note, Marc rose up, "I'll help you," and followed behind her.

Adam was thinking about it all.

"I have to say something," he snapped the soft quiet of the tired folks.

Mardessa had a worried look.

"Please don't, congressman."

"No. I want to apologize for screwing up the party."

Mardessa cringed; dreading all eyes zooming to her.

"No, no," Verdie said. "it ended well. It was a nice night."

Adam sat forward in the chair. "Yeah, but it was me that got the food and just had to have the other side of the family here. I ruined the party."

"No you didn't."

David said, "He begging for a hug."

"Shut up, Dave. I am just saying, sorry. That's it."

"And I am telling you that there is no need to be apologizing," Verdie corrected.

LaQuan sat up.

"The dumb has arisen," Grandmomma said.

"Dude. I am not right," LaQuan said.

"You always wrong."

LaQuan turned and vomited loud over the side of the sofa's arm.

David sat up. "Aw man,"

"Lordie," Verdie exclaimed.

Adam laughed. "Chris Christ, yikes. That don't sound good, and it smells worst."

Mardessa got up and rushed to the bathroom.

Adam looked closer and came to alert. He sees his shoebox was under LaQuan. "No! My shoes. No, man, no!"

David stood up and saw the damage. "Damn, dog. Them shoes is messed up. They special, right? I hope you got the receipt."

Adam was furious but he didn't go too close.

David helped LaQuan up. He tried not to laugh.

"The receipt! You bum! They custom made!"

"Oh no," Verdie said. "The boy threw up on your new shoes?"

LaQuan is drowsy. He said, "I'm okay man. Sorry, Adam, aw, homie. I'm messed up.

"He must have eaten some of food from earlier."

"I tried to tell him not to, but he smarter. And he was mixing drinks all night."

"David, take him to your room and lay him down."

"Okay. Come on champ, the fight is over. You was tough, you just got your ass whipped."

"Shit," Adam now got a look at his shoes. "He can't even afford to pay me for them."

David shook his head while he led LaQuan away. "Why you bring them in here? You should have left them in my room. Show off."

Adam just shook his head.

37

Patricia's stroll was halted by the site of the mess in the kitchen.

"Good," Patricia said. "Now the clean up."

"The best part," Marc scoffed. "You want me to recruit some help?"

"We can handle it, at least get it started."

Patricia moved to the sink. She opened the dishwasher and began loading glasses and snack plates and trays. "You can go home, you know. We going to do most of this tomorrow."

"You want me to leave?"

"If that is how you feel."

"No, I want to help."

He moved to the sink, near Patricia. She felt his eyes. She liked it but kept her eyes on the task at hand.

"You know, I really appreciate you...helping me."

"I know the family has got to be tired."

She had the water running, rinsing off dishes and putting them in the dishwasher like robots, no words between them. Marc didn't allow that routine go on for long. "So, am I going to get an answer tonight?"

Patricia decided she'd deflect the question with a joke. "Grandma and the Chinese saved the party, huh?"

He didn't laugh; she turned to find his eyes ablaze. Was it anger or inquisition? She shrugged. "I don't have an answer."

"What the hell does that mean?"

"See? I don't want to be ordered around."

"What are you talking about?"

"You are moving way too fast for me."

"Too fast?" he said shaking his head. "I am loving you. I want to be with you."

She stopped moving.

"What you think I am a monster or something? Where is this coming from?"

"Don't yell at me."

"This ain't yelling."

"Well keep your voice down." "I'm just saying we have nothing in common. You would turn my life upside down."

"Look, if that is how you feel then just say no and I will leave you alone. How about that? Shit, you have options."

"And where did that come from? Now you cursing at me?"

"Whatever, is what I am saying. I like you and love you."

"There isn't a way to just go backwards. I mean, you propose, rushing things, and we can't go back to being, like, dating."

"Fine. Look. I love being with you. Simple as that. I ain't felt like this in years, with a woman."

"What about baby momma drama."

"No fear of that. She went home to Cincinnati where her family tells her and the kids that they did the right thing in leaving me."

"Why?"

"I wasn't a good man. We were separated two years before the divorce. I didn't want a divorce. What I wanted was a second chance. It didn't come. And now, some years later, it was the right thing. I was a bad husband."

"And now you want to do it again?"

"Yes. That is what I am saying."

David walked in. He saw the seriousness in their eyes; his sister leaning on the sink, arms folded. He spun on his heels and left.

Verdie caught him leaving the kitchen. "Why are you not in there helping your sister."

"She in there with Mr. Marcus."

"And?"

"They having sex, Momma," David said. "In your kitchen."

She shook her head.

With all of the people she loved nearby, Patricia began to thaw. She had to admit she loved his honesty. Marc made good money but she worries how much of his salary would be going to his ex-wife and children.

He said, "Look, forget all the bull. I have feelings for you and I want to be with you. In anyway I can. All that I have been through is experience. I have some knowledge and I know what I want. And that is why I know I love you. "

She had avoided his eyes.

Why hadn't she realized she loved him?

She did. More than her freedom. More than her pride. More than her fears. She loved him. She wanted him. And for the first time she realized it was her own fear that had stood between them this time. He had been afraid to ask her to come. He had been so afraid that when he finally asked, it was only the very end of their time together, which she couldn't say yes without worrying about how genuine his request was.

She had been afraid to tell her he loved her. Love bound people together and then sometimes people left way too early.

She had been a fool.

Arms folded, she said softly, "I am no Susie Homemaker or shrinking violet that needs saving.'

"Like I don't know that? You think that is what I want?"

She was shaking her head, leaning. "I love working. I won't stay home baking and birthing."

"Right, right," he smirked. "Like I said differently?"

She sighed.

"Marry me?"

His hand was on her back. He was mighty close.

"I want to get married. I do."

"You want to marry me?"

She looked into his eyes for the last indication that the love she was feeling, fighting was real. And there it was, clear in his eyes.

"I want to marry you," she finally said.

"Then let's do it."

She smiled, "What did I do to deserve you?"

"Nothing yet," he teased. "But, I'm hoping that you'll prove your worth very soon."

Patricia moved in for a passionate kiss. Marc surrendered.

38

All eyes in the living room shot to the hallway from the kitchen as Patricia and Marc joined them. They found a spot to sit together.

David was half asleep and still he had to say something, Did y'all remove all the nastiness from my momma's kitchen?" He was sitting next to LaQuan, his mouth agape and snoring.

"Shut it up. What about you and your boyfriend."

"Don't make fun of the sleeping."

They all looked at LaQuan drooling and they had to laugh.

Patricia exhaled, "Whew, that was some party. When's Christmas again?"

Adam glared at her from his spot on the couch. He would have reached out and socked her had he not had his wife leaning her head on his shoulder.

It was Verdie's turn to exhale. She said, "You know what, I don't care how tonight is perceived. It was a success in my eyes."

"Who said it was a failure. Point them out and I'll beat them up."

"Calm down, killer." Patricia said.

Verdie went on, "My children got together and in the spirit of the season brought joy to my world."

There were chimes of yeses and nods.

"My children had given me the greatest gift of Christmas, a delighted spirit and a return to the spirit of the holidays. That's all that matters to me. Your father would have loved that the crowd was loud and getting younger. And, shit, I had a good old time."

"Me too, shit," Grandmomma said.

The family laughed, except Grandmomma.

"Now all we need is a wedding," Bebe said.

Verdie looked at her children.

Patricia cringed. This was not the time to discuss it, she was thinking.

David was laughing. "Don't look at me," he said, "I've still yet to be intimately close to Ginata."

"You ain't never going to get that, playboy." That was LaQuan, with his eyes still closed.

Mardessa chuckled at his joke but took in full notice of the affection he had for his girlfriend. She would love to be the first in-law, and she would love to be married this Valentine's Day.

Adam shook his head, not even thinking about the fact he was the only one of Verdie's brood to have given Verdie a wedding to preen over. He knew that his momma wanted it from her only daughter now.

"You know mother dear," Patricia blushed. "Funny that should come up..."

Marc looked into his glass, a grin on his face. He liked that she was going to mention it to everyone now.

"Marc asked me to marry him," she said. She heard the delight in her voice and her grin widened. It wasn't the booze. She looked to Marc and he too was blushing.

Mister Cool is blushing. Yep, she loved him and he loved her too.

"For real?" David grinned.

Patricia kicked him. "Yes, for real."

"What? I am just shocked, that's all."

He was not the most shocked person there.

Verdie was so taken aback that she could not get out the words to ask if her daughter had said yes.

"And you said?" Aunt Bebe asked first instead.

"I was as shocked as the rest of you."

"Damn the shock, let's see the ring?" Aunt Bebe said.

"Ah, no. You will see it if and when I am wearing it."

"Selfish."

Mardessa sipped from her goblet. Oh, she was a bit bitter. She had loved Adam most of her adult life and yet he hadn't asked her to be his wife. What, she did the math, Marc had been courting Tricia for a month. Mardessa avoided looking at Adam. Adam takes Mardessa by her hand into the foyer.

Mardessa so feared what he might be about to say that she choked and her mouth went dry. To be dumped on Christmas would have devastated her.

"I'm sorry." Adam kissed her. "I let this party get me crazy. We are going to work it out, I'm sorry.'

"No, it's okay."

"But look, listen," he tightened his hands over hers, "we'll talk more when we get home. Warm up the car, I have to talk to my brother first."

"Okay, baby."

Adam came back into the living room. "We fixin' to split."

"Aw no," David mocked.

Verdie was a bit disappointed. "Why don't you stay the night? I'm making breakfast."

"We might come back, but we can't stay the night," Adam said. "We have something we need to do tonight."

"Nasty," David grimaced.

"Exactly."

Out of nowhere, LaQuan said, "make up sex, that be the best right there."

"Well, okay then. How does a virgin know, I don't know."

LaQuan put up a middle finger, and the realized what he did. "I'm sorry Miss Verdie."

The brothers hugged tenderly, and David kissed him on the neck.

"Man, I had a fucking good time."

"Well, come see us some time."

"Smart ass."

"You know it. Nothing but love."

Mardessa came back in. "Good night everyone," she said softly.

Verdie came across the kitchen and took Mardessa into a hug, and Patricia, David and Bebe followed. She could feel the night was going to be a horror in the back of her mind for a long time, but the hugs did feel warm and inviting.

"I love you, Momma Verdie."

"I know child, I know. We love you."

And with that Mardessa broke down.

"That damn gin. Told her not to drink so much."

"Shut up," Mardessa smiled through the tears.

"Dude, so you out?"

"Gotta go, gotta go."

"But do me a favor, brother of mine. Since you parked on the side of the house, go out the back door. I got something I got to do up front."

"Cool."

Not more than ten seconds after Adam goes out the back door he let out a scream as he went down hard.

"Ahhhh!"

Everyone rushed to the door and found Adam on his butt.

"Oh, snap, congressman, my bad."

Adam just glared up and shook his head.

"David!" Verdie slapped his arm.

The End

www.ingramcontent.com/pod-product-compliance
Lightning Source LLC
Chambersburg PA
CBHW080807120626
46556CB00009B/3253